D0012448

SUPERHEROES
WITHDRAWN
DON'T EAT veggie BURGERS

BY GRETCHEN KELLEY

HENRY HOLT AND COMPANY   NEW YORK

Henry Holt and Company, LLC
Publishers since 1866
175 Fifth Avenue
New York, New York 10010
mackids.com

Library of Congress Cataloging-in-Publication Data

Kelley, Gretchen.
Superheroes don't eat veggie burgers / Gretchen Kelley.
pages cm
Summary: "A sixth-grade boy's stories about superhero Dude Explodius
start changing reality"—Provided by publisher.
ISBN 978-1-62779-089-5 (hardback)
[1. Ability—Fiction.   2. Superheroes—Fiction.   3. Diaries—Fiction.
4. Middle schools—Fiction.   5. Schools—Fiction.]   I. Title.
II. Title: Superheroes do not eat veggie burgers.
PZ7.1.K42Su 2016   [Fic]—dc23   2015003265

Our books may be purchased in bulk for promotional, educational, or business use. Please
contact your local bookseller or the Macmillan Corporate and Premium Sales Department
at (800) 221-7945 ext. 5442 or by e-mail at MacmillanSpecialMarkets@macmillan.com.

First Edition—2016 / Designed by Anna Booth

Printed in the United States of America
by R. R. Donnelley & Sons Company, Ltd.,
Harrisonburg, Virginia

1 3 5 7 9 10 8 6 4 2

To my children: Mackenzie, Brendan, Sydney, and Riley.
You were my first readers and are my biggest inspiration.

And to my husband, Michael.
You were my first love and are my best friend.

CHAPTER

1

IT'S NOT LIKE I'M LOOKING FOR TROUBLE.

I've just scored two seats in the back of the cafeteria—as far away from the food-fight starters and wedgie-givers as I can get—when I look up to see a kid with armpit hair and a bad case of acne standing over me.

"You call that a sandwich?" he says. A thick finger reaches down and grinds into what was about to be my lunch. Ketchup oozes everywhere.

"What's wrong, pretty boy?" he grunts. "You got something to say?"

What I want to say is that he should consider investing in a toothbrush. Instead I stare at the nutrition facts on the back of my milk carton and pretend to be fascinated by how many grams of protein are in a half pint of chocolate milk.

A raspy voice from across the table answers him for me.

"It's a veggie burger, you idiot."

I look up and cringe. Franki Saylor may be my best friend, but if word gets around Gatehouse Middle School that a girl had to stick up for me on the first day of sixth grade, I might as well write my own death warrant.

The kid shoves me sideways, knocking me off my chair.

"You talking to me, girl?" he growls, pushing his nose up against hers.

"Who else would I be talking to?" she growls back.

I jump up and try wedging myself between them. "Hey . . . uh, it's okay. . . . I wasn't g-going to eat it anyway," I stammer. "I don't even like veggie burgers. I only bring them because my dad—"

"Charlie . . ." Franki says my name like it's a warning, and my stomach tightens in the way that makes me think I've pulled the cord on my gym shorts a little too tight.

Acne Guy looks down at me, a creepy grin sliding across his face.

I start to weigh my options. I could make a run for it, but that'll just call more attention to me. A fake seizure? Probably worse. I know I'm a pretty fast runner, but I'm not too sure about my acting abilities. Maybe if I—

A bell rings and a grown-up's voice booms from the speaker overhead.

"All right, listen up," it demands. "For those of you who

don't know me, I'm your principal, Dr. Daryl Moody, PhD." He spells out the last three letters very slowly, as if we're kindergartners and his first order of business is to review the alphabet with us. A couple of kids boo, while someone throws a half-eaten bagel at the ceiling. "For those of you who don't *wish* to know me, I suggest you get moving. Fifth period starts in exactly three minutes. Now scram."

The kid pulls his finger out of my sandwich.

"This ain't over, Goldilocks," he says, flicking one of my curls. I feel a spray of ketchup hit my ear and start dripping down my neck.

"Hey!" Franki warns, but I shoot her a look that thankfully shuts her up.

I swat at the glob hanging from my earlobe and realize I've just learned my first lesson at Gatehouse Middle School.

Even the wrong sandwich can put a guy in the hot seat.

And then, as I feel a pair of meaty hands grab my gym shorts and yank them south, I learn my second one.

Never show up at middle school if you're not wearing underwear.

CHAPTER

2

"CHARLIE! DO SOMETHING!"

Franki's voice sounds warbly and faraway, like it does when it's summer, we're swimming in Mill Pond, and she's trying to tell me a dirty joke underwater.

But we're not at Mill Pond.

And this is definitely no joke.

I crouch down and grab for my shorts just as Franki dives across the table, coating her arms and legs in ketchup and spaghetti sauce. By the time I get everything back in place, she's standing next to me, looking like she just got back from a war zone.

A quick peek over my shoulder confirms my worst fear: A gazillion googly eyes stare back at us. Mouths hang open like cellar doors with busted hinges. And except for the ticktock of an old metal clock that hangs over the salad bar, the room has gone silent. I stare down at the orange swoosh on my too-new Nikes and wait for the world to end.

Franki grabs my shoulder. "You okay?" she barks.

I push her away from me, hard. "Jeez, Frank," I hiss, "try not to make this any worse, okay?"

Somebody in front of us makes a smoochy sound, while another kid starts giggling.

"All right, show's over." Franki waves her arms around like she's preparing to conduct an orchestra. "Get moving, everyone."

The mob explodes in laughter.

That's it—I can't take any more. Ducking under her bony elbow, I push my way through the crowd, ignoring the whistles and catcalls, even ignoring my best friend, who keeps hollering for me to wait up.

I make it to the double doors right as the bell rings. I shove them open and run.

■ ■ ■

It doesn't take long for her to find me.

I'm holed up in the first-floor boys' bathroom, third stall, my legs tucked up to my chin. I don't know how long I've been sitting like that—five minutes? twenty? an hour?—when I hear her voice, snaking around the urinals and under the stall door.

"Charlie? You in there?"

I squeeze my arms around my legs and hold my breath.

"I'm not afraid to come into the boys' bathroom, you know."

I can't help smiling at this. After five years of doing everything together, I know that Franki Saylor isn't afraid of anything. Hiding from her is no use. She'll find me eventually. She always does.

I heave myself off the can and unlatch the stall door. She walks into the bathroom right as I'm shuffling up to the row of yellow-stained sinks, and watches while I flip on the first faucet.

After a minute, she leans back against the tile wall and clears her throat.

"Can we just drop it, Frank?" I ask. I run my hands under the water and grab a paper towel. I don't bother with soap.

Her face breaks into her lopsided grin, showing me the hole where she lost her fourteenth tooth last week while we were clam digging at Good Harbor Beach. We buried it alongside a half-mangled starfish, since the Tooth Fairy stopped showing up at Franki's house years ago.

"No, we can't just drop it." She blows a piece of hair out of her face. "I've got the perfect plan for getting Boomer back for what he did to you—"

"Boomer?" Uh-oh. The drawstring is tightening around my gut again.

"Yeah, Boomer Bodbreath," she says. "He's the kid who pantsed you. You know who he is, don't you?"

"Of course I know who he is." I try to make my voice sound normal. "But he's supposed to be in high school this year."

Her eyes twinkle like they do when she's about to let me in on something big.

"Got held back. They're making him repeat eighth grade." She slaps me on the back. "So, here's my plan. . . ."

I turn from the sink and glare up at her. Franki may be taller than I am, but my dad says I'm catching up fast. "Listen, Frank," I say. "I got my own plan. And you want to know what it is?" I don't wait for her to answer. "It's to stay as far away from guys like Boomer as possible. I don't need to get back at him. In fact, I don't need to get back at anyone. I just want to make it through sixth grade in one piece. Got it?"

I lob the paper towel over her head but miss the trash can.

"Charlie." She says my name in a whisper-voice that makes the inside of my chest go all achy. "If somebody doesn't put a stop to guys like Boomer, they end up doing way worse things than just pantsing people."

I look at her, the dried ketchup stuck to her forehead and tiny spaghetti sauce splotches dotting her favorite Green Day T-shirt, and shudder. Franki's plans have a way of putting both of us in the spotlight, a place I do not want to be this year.

"That's great, Frank," I tell her, "but that somebody isn't going to be me."

She stares at me for a second, then turns and walks back toward the bathroom door, slapping both palms against it.

She starts to push on it, then stops. She spins around, the excitement of her plan drained from her face.

"You know what your problem is, Charlie Burger?" she says, glaring.

I glare back better. "No, Frank . . . but I bet you're going to tell me."

"Your problem," she says, pushing the door so wide that everyone in the hallway can hear, "is that you've got a lot of heart—but zero guts."

She swings out of the bathroom, and I kick the wall so hard, my left big toe hurts for the rest of the day.

CHAPTER

SHOWING UP LATE TO FIFTH PERIOD IS NOT going to help me stay out of the spotlight. Especially since I'm now the Just-Got-Pantsed Guy.

I think about sicking out and heading to the nurse's office, but decide against it. She'll probably insist on calling my dad, who will show up with a protein shake and a van full of his homemade veggie burgers that still need to be delivered. My dad is a caterer, and almost every house on Cape Ann orders a dozen of his famous veggie burgers, baked beans, and organic coleslaw for their backyard and beach cookouts. So even though it would be great to have him all to myself for a few hours, I'd have to ride shotgun while he made his runs around the cape, and we'd spend the whole time discussing my poor eating habits and how my stomachaches would go away if I'd just make healthier choices.

No thanks. I'd rather deal with a bunch of gawking sixth graders than hear that lecture again.

Standing in the doorway of the science lab, I scope out the room. Four guys in the back are engaged in an all-out spitball war, while a group of girls in the middle huddle together, giggling and smearing shiny stuff on their lips. The nerds are at the front table, their heads already buried in books, clueless to what's going on around them.

I've just spied the last empty seat near the back when a man in a gray cowboy hat and perfectly pressed blue jeans saunters up behind me.

"Howdy, pardner," he says, nodding at me. A large cardboard box fills his arms, the bottom looking like it's going to bust wide open at any minute.

Everyone stops what they're doing. Even the nerds look up from their books, curious.

He waits for me to say something.

"Uh . . . hi," I mumble, craning my neck up to see his face. It reminds me of a piece of beef jerky.

"I reckon you're Charlie Burger," he says.

I blink at him. "You already know my name?"

He smiles, his eyes crinkling at the corners. They twinkle like they hold a special secret.

"I guess I do," he says. "I'm Mr. Perdzock, your sixth-grade science teacher. Most kids call me Mr. P for short." We stand there for a full minute—him looking me up and down, and me thinking maybe I should've gotten a haircut this summer.

"Had a little trouble in the lunchroom, I hear," he says. His eyes grow darker, like the ocean right before a Nor'easter blows in.

Someone snickers, and Mr. P's head snaps up, scanning the room. No one moves.

"Well, no sense worrying about that now." He looks back down at me, and his face seems to soften a little, even though his eyes stay the same. "A little adversity is good for a guy, right, pardner? Keeps us in the saddle, so to speak."

Pardner? Saddle? It's like this guy just stepped out of one of those John Wayne Westerns my grandmother likes to watch.

When I don't say anything, he points toward an empty chair at the front table. "Why don't you mosey on over there and join the rest of the class." I have to climb over an out-stretched leg, and I practically trip over someone's backpack before plopping myself down smack-dab in the middle of the front row. A chubby girl with greasy hair and a bad sunburn sits next to me.

"Loser," she whispers under her breath. I stare at her like, *Who're you kidding?* She rolls her eyes at me and looks away.

"All right now, where was I?" Mr. P asks.

The chubby girl raises her hand. "You were telling us you had something important to hand out." She waggles her big bottom like she's a superstar for having remembered this, and I have to bite my lip to keep from laughing. I have a feeling I don't want to be on her bad side.

"Yes, right. Stay focused, Perdzock," he says to himself. He glances around the room, then sets the box down. "Your writing journals." He pulls out a pile of dark leather notebooks and starts walking down the aisles, slapping one in front of each of us, the heels of his cowboy boots click-clacking on the tile floor. "Make sure you put your name on the cover." He stops when he gets to me. "You don't want to lose these."

I pull a pencil out of my backpack as he continues, "Everyone in this room has a story to tell. These journals will be an important part of your first . . . experiment." His voice is slow and thick, like maple syrup. "And who knows? Maybe your experiment will be the one to change the world."

He drops a notebook in front of me.

"Or," he says, winking, "at least make it an easier place for a few folks."

I sneak a glance at Grant Gupta, who is my second best friend after Franki. Grant is the best striker on our soccer team and has been the school-wide spelling bee champ since third grade. He's also the shortest kid in our class and wears glasses as thick as the bottom of a soda bottle.

A hand shoots up across from me. It's Dolores Bryant's, the self-appointed Queen of the Nerds. Anybody who wants to keep a low profile knows to steer clear of her. "I have a question. Quite a few, in fact." She stares down at something in front of her. A list, I bet.

Mr. P pulls a toothpick from his pocket and nods at her. "I like questions," he says, popping it into his mouth. "Shoot."

"Yes, well . . . can you tell us how exactly this journal will be graded? Do you have a syllabus, or some sort of rubric? I'll definitely need a rubric." Groans are heard around the classroom, but Dolores ignores them. "I am planning on going to medical school, and this class is very important to me."

A spitball flies past my ear and lodges itself in the back of Dolores's braid. Whistles are heard from the back row.

Mr. P puts his hands out as if he's stopping traffic.

"Now listen up, y'all," he says, rolling the toothpick around with his tongue, "there is no rubric for this assignment, only one rule, you hear?" He surveys the room, his eyes growing cloudier. "You've got to write stories that come from your gut."

My own gut doesn't feel so good. What's wrong with this guy? We're supposed to be dissecting frogs and mixing chemicals, not writing stories in some stupid journal. I look around to see if anyone else is as weirded out as I am, but if they are, they're sure not showing it.

He balls his hand into a fist and pushes it against his

stomach. "I want you to open those gates and let your imaginations run as wild as a pack of ponies on a wide-open prairie. Set your ideas free, and see where they take you."

The bell rings, and everyone grabs their book bags, stuffing the journals inside. As I pick up mine, a sharp jolt of electricity zips up my arm and through the hairs on the back of my neck, making me drop the journal to the floor. Mr. P bends over and picks it up.

"You like writing, son?"

I shrug. "It's not my favorite subject."

He nods. "More of a science guy, huh?"

"Science just makes more sense to me."

He smiles, and the cracks and crevices on his cheeks grow even deeper. "I want you to listen to me carefully, Charlie. A true scientist won't spend time on the things that make sense. He will ask questions about the things that don't. And even when he's figured out the answers to those questions, he still won't be completely satisfied. He'll always come up with more."

I'm trying to make sense of what he's saying, but the room is getting hot, and Grant's standing in the doorway, waving at me to hurry up. No one wants to get caught talking to a teacher, especially not on the first day of school.

"Mr. P, if I don't hurry—"

He holds the journal out to me. "Words can be powerful. Believe in their magic and anything can happen." His eyes sparkle like someone lit a firecracker behind them. "Do you believe in magic, Charlie?"

I blink. "You mean, like card tricks and stuff?"

"Not exactly," he says, moving his toothpick from one side of his mouth to the other. "You better get a move on. No sense in being late to another class."

CHAPTER

"SO, HOW WAS IT?" MY DAD ASKS AS I SLIDE open the door of his minivan and dive in, face-planting onto a leftover veggie burger.

A voice from the backseat answers for me.

"Charlie got pantsed at school today," my little sister singsongs, bouncing up and down on her seat. "And . . . guess what else."

"Here we go," I mutter into the burger. Lucy's only in fifth grade but always manages to know stuff, especially if it's about me.

"My brother," she says, so loud that I bet even the lobstermen down at the wharf can hear, "wasn't wearing any *underwear!*"

Even though I can't see his face, I'm pretty sure my dad is grinning. "Charlie?"

"I couldn't find a clean pair," I mumble.

"I mean, come *on*," Lucy continues. "What kind of moron doesn't wear underwear to school? Especially *middle school!*"

I look up and shoot her my most evil stink eye, wishing for the millionth time in my almost twelve years of life that Lucy Burger had never been born.

The passenger door flies open, and my older sister climbs in, waving to her gang of groupies like they've just crowned her Miss Massachusetts.

"Did you hear, Stella?" Lucy bounces higher, eager for as much attention as she can get. "Did you hear the big news?"

Oh, great. The last thing I need is the Queen of Coolness knowing about this. "Lucy," I say, shaking my fist in her face. "If you say another—"

Stella turns and flashes her bright-white smile in my direction. "Getting pantsed isn't a big deal, Charlie," she says. "It happens."

Like she would know. No one would even think about pantsing Stella Burger. She's been on the student council for three years in a row and on the dance team for two. She's so bent on becoming the most popular person ever to walk the halls of Gatehouse Middle School, I'm surprised she can even remember my name.

My dad pulls the van away from the curb and looks at me in the rearview mirror. "So . . . how was the rest of your day?"

"Weird," I say.

"Weird?"

"Yeah," I say, shaking my head. "It's just . . . well, science class wasn't exactly what I thought it would be."

His eyebrows shoot to the top of his forehead. "But you love science."

I come from a long line of scientists. My great-grandfather was a chemist who helped create nitroglycerin, which was later used to make dynamite. My grandpa Burger was a chemistry professor at Harvard. According to my dad, Gramps never invented anything but was willing to "die trying." Whenever I ask what that means, my dad gets this pinched look on his face and says it doesn't really matter, because things worked out for the best. Which I guess is sort of true, since instead of becoming a scientist, my dad went to cooking school and invented a veggie burger that's so popular, people drive from all over New England just to eat one. A Burger's Best Veggie Burger is a local favorite around Cape Ann.

Still, I think I'd rather invent stuff that blows up than a burger made of bean sprouts. I guess that's just me.

"It's my science teacher," I say, digging a half-eaten box of Nerds out from under my seat. "He gave us these journals and told us that we're supposed to write stories in them instead of lab reports. And . . ." I mumble, "he looks like he's older than dirt and just stepped out of the Wild Wild West."

Stella kicks off her sandals and laughs.

"Oh . . . you got Mr. P," she says, putting her feet on the dashboard. "I never had him, but I've heard he does the same thing every year—hands out a bunch of fancy leather notebooks to all his sixth graders, then tells them stuff like, 'Your stories will change the world,' and 'Writing is magical,' right?" She studies a bright-pink toenail. "Don't worry—he'll disappear around fall break and come back ready to teach science."

"Disappear?" My dad glances over at her, then back at the road. "Where does he go?"

Stella shrugs. "Somewhere exotic, like the Caribbean or Cambodia . . . I don't really pay attention to stuff like that."

"So what happens to the journal writing?" I ask. Maybe things are looking up.

"*Finito,*" she says, picking off a piece of polish. "Everyone says that eventually he loses interest in the whole writing thing and starts teaching about gravitational pull and the speed of light . . . junk like that."

Great, I think—staring out the window as we pass the wharf, Wowee Hair Salon, and Hampton's Hardware—two months of torture before we get down to the good stuff. What a waste.

My dad glances back at me again. "Cheer up, Charlie. In

celebration of your first day of middle school, I'm cooking meat tonight."

I sit up straighter. "Are you saying what I think you're saying?"

He nods. "You betcha, buddy. Bacon lasagna cooked to order by yours truly." Having a dad who's a vegetarian chef means meat gets cooked in our house only on special occasions.

"Ewww," says Lucy. "Animal flesh is revolting."

"Hey now," says my dad, turning off the main street and onto our narrower one. "This is a special day for your brother." He winks at me. "First day of middle school means lots more responsibility, right, son?"

I force the corners of my mouth to turn up.

"Maybe he could start with being responsible enough to put on underwear," murmurs Lucy.

"Button it, freak show," I tell her.

She leans up against the seat, and I can smell her strawberry lip gloss. "Just because I am two years ahead of my class in math and a way better soccer player than you doesn't make me a freak, Charlie," she says, batting her eyelashes at me. "It makes me gifted. Big difference, buddy boy. Big."

"All right, you two. Enough." My dad pulls into our gravel driveway and cuts the engine. "Everyone, out."

Lucy and I unbuckle at the same time, then race for the

mailbox. I get there first, lift open the front flap, and snatch out the envelopes, holding them high above my head so she has to jump for them. It's a battle we've waged for years.

But today, something other than a bill or a piece of junk mail falls out of the pile and drops onto my sneaker. It's a regular envelope, but right away I recognize the gold seal in the corner and the return address: Cape Ann Soccer Academy, Gloucester, MA.

Lucy stops jumping.

I flip it over, and my stomach does a flip, too. It's addressed to me, Charles Michael Burger.

Lucy's mouth hangs open, her eyes all buggy. "You got the Letter."

Stella, who had been walking with my dad, stops and turns to us, her face looking like she just took a swig of sour milk. Even though Stella couldn't care less about soccer, she knows what this means. Rejections from the academy come in the mail. Acceptances come over the phone.

"Open it," Lucy demands.

"Nope," I say.

Lucy stomps the ground, her curls bouncing like springs on her shoulders.

"Come on, Charlie. I promise I won't—"

A sudden string of four-letter words from the front porch cuts her off. We both turn in time to see my dad's grocery bag split open. Onions, celery, and a bag of organic apples spill onto the front porch. My special-occasion bacon lies in a puddle of goat's milk.

Stella rushes to help, and I make a run for it.

"Charlie, wait up!" Lucy may be a better soccer player, but I can beat her in a footrace any day. I cut to the left, swing around the side of the house, and hightail it for the back door. Darting through the kitchen, I snag an oatmeal cookie from the fresh stack on the counter and then beeline it for the stairs, taking them two at a time.

I make it to my room and slam the door behind me, but my victory is bittersweet.

Stuffing the cookie in my mouth, I rip open the envelope. Right away I see the first line: *We regret to inform you* . . .

Shoving a pile of dirty clothes off my bed, I flop down and cover my face with the letter. I stay like that until it no longer smells like fresh ink.

Trying out for the academy was my mom's idea, not mine. She said that I should give it a try, that it would help me stretch outside my comfort zone, take a risk, stuff like that. But I knew I wasn't good enough to make it—as much as I knew Lucy was.

"Charlie?"

I sit up, and the paper floats to the floor. My dad stands in the doorway, holding his cell phone in one hand and a wooden spoon in the other, which drips a dark brown liquid down the front of his KISS ME, I'M VEGAN apron. His face tells me the news.

22

"She made it, didn't she?" I ask. "Lucy got a spot on the academy team."

He presses his lips together, hard. "Listen, Charlie . . ."

"It's no big deal, Dad," I say, jumping up and walking over to my desk. "I'll just play for the middle-school team. They stink so bad, they'll be thrilled to have me."

"Charlie." Now he's frowning. "You're as good a soccer player as the next guy."

"That's not what they think," I say, scuffing my foot on the piece of paper. "That's not what Mom thinks."

My dad sighs and rubs his head with the dripping spoon.

"That's not fair, Charlie. Your mom just wants to see you live up to your potential," he says. "We both want you to be the best you can be."

I run the toe of my sneaker along the scratches in the floorboards, carved deep from years of soccer cleats and Matchbox cars. "Yeah, well, maybe this is my best. Maybe this is as good as it gets."

Dad leans over and puts both of his hands on my shoulders. His eyes are see-through green, like mine. "Part of growing up is taking responsibility for yourself, Charlie. If you want something bad enough, you've got to put your mind to getting it. And remember, there's always next year, right?"

For some reason this makes me feel worse, but I smile anyway.

"Sure, Dad," I say. "Next year."

His face loosens. Standing up straight, he pats me on the back and then starts toward the door.

"That's the spirit! Now, why don't you get started on your homework? Your mom will be home soon, and then we'll have dinner." He turns around and grins at me. "You're still in the mood for bacon lasagna, right?"

I nod, then listen as his footsteps head down the hall toward Lucy's room. I hear a light rap on her door. I press my palms against my ears, but her eardrum-splitting scream at the good news is unavoidable.

Flopping backward onto my bed, I stare up at the ceiling and think about what Mr. P said earlier today.

Words can be powerful. Believe in their magic and anything can happen.

I sit up and reach for my backpack on the floor. Pulling out the science notebook, I flip to the first page and start writing.

September 8
The Adventures of Dude Explodius, Ruler of Everything
By Charlie Burger
Episode 1: The Greatest Dude Alive

Even through the darkness that surrounded him, his superhuman vision allowed him to take it all in: the ten-story compound that had been built specifically for him, the regulation-size soccer field and dodgeball court where he always got to pick his team first, and the cozy cafeteria where seating was limited to a select few and his favorite foods were only a command away. Sitting on top of his custom-made beanbag chair, he smiled, satisfied that all was as it should be on Planet Splodii—his planet, his domain.

He had too many powers to count. After all, he was not just a superhero—he was a super<u>dude</u>: Dude Explodius, Ruler of Everything.

It didn't get any better than that.

He had ruled Planet Splodii for as long as anyone could remember. Stories of his remarkable strength, skill, and pure awesomeness were shared from generation to generation, not to mention his geniuslike intellect, amazing athleticism, and jaw-dropping good looks. Girls adored him, guys worshipped him, and any creature with half a brain knew to stay on his good side. That went for his enemies as well as the people of Splodii.

He was, after all, a generous ruler.

Except when forced to be otherwise.

CHAPTER

WHEN YOU LIVE IN A BEACH TOWN, THE BEST
Saturdays of summer come after Labor Day.

I wake up early and look around my room. My backpack sits next to my desk, where I dropped it after school yesterday. I pick it up and shove it into my closet. I've just made it through my first four days of middle school. I'm not planning on looking at that thing until Monday.

Now that the tourists have all gone back to Boston and the lifeguards have all left for college, Franki and I will have the beach to ourselves—which is how we like it best. We'll spend the morning checking out the tide pools and climbing the rock faces, since no one's around to tell us not to. After lunch I'll talk my dad into biking to Mill Pond with us, since his catering business slows way down after tourist season.

We'll hunt frogs in the marsh around the pond and fish for black crappies until it gets too dark to see our hooks and my dad starts worrying that someone is going to stick one through a finger. Franki did that once, and believe me, it wasn't a pretty sight.

I pick up a T-shirt off my floor and sniff it. *Not bad*, I decide, and pull it over my head. As I tiptoe past Lucy's room, I pray she's still asleep. Luckily, it works: Forty million stuffed animals stand sentry around the lump in her bed, and a thick trail of drool slides out of the corner of her mouth and onto her bright-pink pillowcase. I resist the urge to sneak in and dunk one of her curls into the slobber pool. If I wake her, my plans are toast.

I bolt downstairs and inhale a bowl of Froot Loops before anyone's awake. My dad thinks processed cereals are equivalent to poison, but my mom buys them anyway. She tries to support my dad's healthy habits, but it's pretty obvious she thinks he takes things a little too far.

Next, a pit stop at the bathroom. No one's around, so I don't lift the seat. My aim is always spot-on. Almost always.

With the coast clear, I jump down the basement stairs two at a time and leap over the banister. I grab the remote off the side table, vault the cushions, and *bam!* The screen comes to life before my butt even hits the couch.

Dude Explodius would be proud, I think, and I can't help but chuckle over the ingenious plan I came up with for my science journal. Sure, a bunch of made-up adventures about an imaginary superhero aren't really going to change the world, but hopefully, they'll keep this Mr. P off my back until he takes off for that exotic place. Afterward he'll come back and teach me some stuff that matters.

Thinking about the first adventure I wrote makes my fingers start to tingle again, like they did in science class. I look down at my hand, but it's the same hand I've had for the last eleven years. I shrug and click through the television channels until I land on an old X-Men episode and think about what Dude would be doing on a Saturday morning, and what he'd eat for breakfast—salami, probably, and a T-bone steak. I close my eyes. He'd wash it down with a tall glass of—

"I want to watch something else."

I open my eyes. Lucy stands in front of me, hands on her hips. Her hair hangs perfectly in tiny ringlets around her shoulders, and a gigantic pink bow perches on top of her head. She's wearing her favorite soccer jersey and a frilly purple skirt. Lucy refuses to wear pants or shorts, even when she's playing soccer.

I can't believe it. Ten minutes ago, the kid was drooling in her sleep.

"Get out of here, Lucy."

She crosses her arms.

"That show is too violent. Mom says."

I wave the remote at her. "Too violent for babies. So scram."

She sits down on the edge of the couch, spreading her skirt out around her like a fan.

"Let's watch *Princess Academy*."

"Can't you bug someone else for once?"

She twirls a curl around her finger. "Everyone else is busy."

"Go call a friend."

"No one's answering."

Lucy may be smart at math and good at soccer, but she's pretty lousy at making friends. My mom says her peers haven't learned to appreciate her leadership skills, and my dad says she needs time to grow into her personality. I think she's just a prissy know-it-all whose classmates are sick of her bossing them around.

She lets out a dramatic sigh. "Change the channel now, and I won't tell Mom you've got your feet on the couch."

"I'm going to say it one more time," I tell her. "Get. Out."

She scoots closer. "Make me."

I shove her with my foot. She wails like I stuck her with a cattle prod.

"You touched me!" she shrieks. "You probably haven't washed those things in a week."

"You're right," I tell her, wiggling my toes in her face. "And I walked barefoot through Mr. Everson's yard yesterday." I duck as she hurls a couch pillow toward me. "That place is swimming in dog turds."

"I'm telling. I'm so telling," she cries, jumping up to head back upstairs. "When Mom hears about this, you're going to be oh-so-sorry."

"You're going to be oh-so-sorry," I mimic, turning back toward the TV. Less than a minute later, my mom's voice fills the basement.

"Charles Burger!" I look over at the clock on the table next to me. It's not even ten. Doesn't that woman ever sleep in?

"Charlie?"

I sink lower into the couch cushions.

"Charles, I know you're down there. Front and center, buster."

This is the part I don't understand. Why is it that she's allowed to stand at the top of the staircase and holler for me, but when I do it, I get the don't-you-dare-yell-at-me-like-that speech?

Maybe I should try it on her.

Hey, Mom! I'd call out. *I'm sitting on my butt watching Cyclops try not to get annihilated by Apocalypse, so if you have something to say, you're gonna have to come down here and say it to my face.*

Yeah, right.

I aim the remote at the screen and flop back on the cushions, thinking about what Mr. P said, how words can be powerful and that if I believed in their magic, anything could happen.

Anything? I wonder.

"Charlie!" Lucy's voice bellows down the stairs. "Mom says now!"

I sigh and drag myself off the couch. Who am I kidding? I don't even have power over my bratty kid sister.

■ ■ ■

Upstairs, three sets of brown eyes stare at me.

My mom stands in the kitchen doorway, flanked by my sisters.

I point at Lucy. "She started it."

My mom peers over her glasses, her thumbs hooked in her belt loops. "Why didn't you tell me about this?"

I scratch my head, which still feels full of sleep.

"I'm not kidding around, young man."

Here's the thing about my mom—she never kids around. I don't know if it's because she's a cop or a mom, but this lady is an expert interrogator.

"I didn't really walk barefoot through Mr. Everson's yard," I say. "I just wanted her to leave me alone."

My mom raises her eyebrow. "What does that have to do with the festival?"

I sneak a peek at Stella, hoping she'll give me a clue as to what's going on.

"The fall festival, Charlie," Stella says, poking me. "It's in a week. We really need more participation this year, and you promised you'd talk it up with the other sixth graders, remember?"

Right. Like that's something I'm going to keep in my frontal cortex.

"Oh yeah, about that . . ." I reach for a powdered doughnut, but my mom shakes her head.

"You already had Froot Loops. I saw the bowl in the sink," she says. Jeez, this lady doesn't miss a beat. "If you're going to this festival thing, you'll need a haircut. And a decent shirt." She looks me up and down like I'm in a lineup. "I mean really, Charlie. You're in middle school now. It's time to put a little more effort into your appearance."

"Aww, Mom, my appearance is fine. And my hair is—"

She wags her finger. "Just a trim. If we leave soon, we'll have time to get to the mall and back before Lucy's soccer practice."

The mall? Surely, she's joking.

"It's my first practice with the academy," Lucy singsongs, twirling around the kitchen.

"Mom, Franki and I have plans today."

"Well, can't you reschedule for tomorrow? This is my only day off this week, and I want to spend it with my children." She turns toward the sink. "Is that too much to ask?"

Lucy hugs her around the waist. "I love spending time with you."

"Suck-up," I mutter.

"Mom!" Lucy's shriek makes my eyes water. "Did you hear what he just said?"

"Knock it off, both of you." My mom sighs and swipes white doughnut powder off the countertop. "And, Charlie? Could you put on a different shirt? It looks like you slept in that one."

She leaves the kitchen, and Stella trails behind her, pleading her case for why she needs a new pair of skinny jeans. I glance at Lucy, who swipes another doughnut while nobody's looking.

Groaning, I slink toward the laundry room, knowing Dude would never get roped in to spending a Saturday at the mall.

■ ■ ■

Three hours, five stores, and one haircut later, we're back in my mom's squad car, about to head home. Stella always gets shotgun, which leaves me crammed in the back with you-know-who.

"You know, Charlie," Lucy says, waving her Barbie doll in my face. "There's going to be dancing at the festival. With slow songs. My friend Evie told me."

"Evie's not your friend anymore," I say. "Remember when you made her cry at the pool because you wouldn't quit calling her four-eyes?"

"She's just sensitive," she says, smoothing down her doll's hair. "She'll get over it."

I'm about to say something else, but I stop when I see my mom watching us in the rearview mirror. Her mood has soured since breakfast.

The mall always does this to her. She says that as an officer of the law, it's her job to be on the lookout for criminal mischief, even when not on duty. Unfortunately, her judgment is sometimes off.

"I could have sworn I saw that girl put a tube of lipstick in her purse," she says as we pull out of our parking space. "It was an honest mistake on my part."

"Mom, she *did* put it in her purse," Stella says, letting her head flop back on the seat. "But she also had a receipt, which she tried to show you while you were dragging her down the hall, screaming for the store manager."

"Escorted her," my mom points out. "I didn't drag. I escorted. And the store manager could have shown me a little more appreciation."

"Whatever, Mom." Stella sighs, taking a swig of her Diet Coke. "The point is, she had the receipt and was trying to explain to you that she only wanted to be earth friendly when she told the salesgirl she didn't need a bag."

My mom starts chewing her thumbnail, but Stella continues. "That's not even the worst part, though. The worst part is that the person you tried to get arrested was Sara Martelli!"

Stella's voice has taken on a screechy quality, and her face is getting all blotchy, something she can't stand.

I don't know Sara Martelli. But I do know it's pretty embarrassing when your mom insists on grabbing random people and dragging them into a store manager's office or her squad car every time she thinks they're up to no good.

We ride in silence for a good minute before Lucy starts in on me again.

"Maybe a girl will actually want to dance with you at the festival. A real girl. Not one like Franki. A girl you might want to *kiss*." She shoves her Barbie in my face, making a sucking sound with her lips.

"Shut up, drain-brain," I hiss, swatting the doll away. "When I want your opinion, I'll ask for it."

My mom shoots me a look. "You know, Charles, this festival is going to be a great opportunity for you to meet some new people, expand your horizons. . . ." Her voice trails off, and I wonder what kind of horizons a crummy middle-school dance could possibly offer me.

"Yeah," chimes in Lucy, "seeing as how you only have one real friend." She leans away from me, knowing what's coming next.

Thwack! I don't punch her hard, but she howls like I hit her with a dump truck. My mom slams her foot on the brakes, causing Stella's Diet Coke to spill all over her brand-new skinny jeans. Mom puts the car in park.

"Really, Charlie?" My mom gives me the one-eyebrow-raised look in the rearview mirror. "Don't you think you're too old for this kind of behavior?" She shakes her head. "It's about time you start growing up."

Stella glares at me over her shoulder as my mom puts the car in drive and creeps up Beach Street, obeying the twenty-five-mile-an-hour speed limit.

For the rest of the way home, Lucy rubs her shoulder, my mom continues to bite at her thumbnail, and Stella dabs at her new dark-washed jeans with a tissue. I watch the seagulls on the beach scavenge what's left from the summer, and wonder what Dude would do if he had a crummy sister like Lucy Burger.

September 13
Episode 2: The King of the Castle

Dude peeked around the corner. His mind-meld powers were working overtime today. The Imbecile stood in the kitchen, preparing Dude's favorite meal: Froot Loops, bacon, and powdered doughnuts covered in warm chocolate sauce. A large glass of milk, ice-cold, was already waiting on the tray that she would bring him when summoned.

She looked up as he entered the room.

"Good morning, sir," she called out. "Your breakfast is almost ready. Would you like me to bring it down to you?"

He grunted a quick response, which she knew to take as a yes.

"Yes, sir. And, sir? Will you be needing a shower today?"

He looked at her as if she were nuts. Had she forgotten about his hygienic manipulation powers? The need to shower, brush his teeth, and cut his toenails did not exist for him. Basic grooming was something for less intelligent life-forms to deal with.

As she realized her error, her face turned crimson. She started to apologize for her mistake, but he gave her a small smile, which seemed to relax her. She was, after all, his most loyal servant and clearly worshipped the ground he walked on. It would be a shame to get rid of her just because of one small slipup.

He slid past her and down the shiny banister into the Cave, his supersecret, private hangout where all of the latest gaming devices and electronic gadgets were at his fingertips. He plunked himself onto the overstuffed couch and snapped his fingers. The ginormous flat-screen HD plasma television with surround sound blinked to life in front of him, a seventy-two-inch SpongeBob filling the screen. Ready for hours of his favorite cartoons, Dude sank back into the cushions, knowing no one would dare to bother him down here.

No one with half a brain, that is. Five minutes into his favorite episode, the Imbecile appeared, carrying a tray. She stared at him, wide-eyed, obviously in awe of the powerful figure sitting in front of her.

"I have brought your breakfast, sir," she whispered. "May I place it in front of you?"

"Yes, put it there," he instructed, pointing to the table in front of him.

The Imbecile smiled as if she could not believe her good fortune. She set down the tray, then bowed in front of him.

"Anything for you, sir."

Dude looked at her, an idea forming in his head. He squeezed his eyes shut and concentrated. After a moment he could feel it happening.

He opened his eyes. Where the Imbecile had once been, there was now a dog.

A big dog.

"Wroof!" it barked, and wagged its tail.

Dude sat back and reached for a piece of just-right bacon, pleased with his creation.

"I'll call you Bill."

He'd always wanted a dog.

CHAPTER

6

I HATE IT WHEN LUCY'S RIGHT.

Well, she's not totally right. Technically, I do have more than one friend. I've got Grant, who's been playing on the same soccer team as I have since we were seven, and playing chess against me since we were nine. And then there's Willy Drozdov, whose dad owns the butcher shop next to the police station where I sometimes hang out. Plus, I guess you could count Anthony Gargotti, even though we don't see each other very often. His dad is on the police force with my mom, but I only see him at company cookouts and stuff. He goes to a different school, one for special kids, according to my dad.

"*One for juvenile delinquents,*" according to my mom.

Okay, so maybe I'm not winning awards in the popularity

department, but I'm fine with that. Because having a friend like Franki is like having five friends all rolled into one.

The first time I met Franki was the summer after kindergarten, when we tied for first place in the summer reading program at the public library. My dad invited her to walk to the Sweet Spot with us, where we both ordered Dinosaur Crunch ice cream with sprinkles and spent the rest of the afternoon comparing favorite books and the scabs we'd scored from climbing trees in Dinwiddy Park.

We've been best friends ever since.

We eat lunch together every day and love to dip our Cheetos in ranch dressing. Both of us would rather read a book than talk to most people. During the summer, Franki practically lives at my house, except when her mom works late and she has to babysit her little sister, Rose. And even though Cemetery Hill is creepier than any horror movie, we're willing to use it as a cut-through because it's the fastest way to each other's house.

Stella says that middle school will change Franki and me and that I shouldn't count on things staying the same. When I tell her that Franki and I are different, she pats me on the head and says someday I'll understand.

But I don't buy it. Franki and I are going to be best friends forever.

"Hey, Chuck!"

I look up, and my mouth drops open. It's Monday

morning, and Franki's already standing at our meeting spot. Usually, it's me standing here, craning my neck up the hill, sure she's going to make us late and I'll have to go to the office for a tardy slip. Then, right when I'm ready to give up, she'll come flying toward me, her hair like a bright-orange sail spread out wide behind her. She'll screech to a halt, and her lopsided grin will make it hard for me to be mad at her for making me wait so long.

Plus, she always has some reason: One time, her little sister, Rose, threw up on Franki's favorite sneakers, and they couldn't find another pair. Another time, her stepdad had polished off the last of the cereal for dinner, so she had to make pancakes instead. Her excuses may not be great, but I'm willing to be late just so I can hear them.

But today, she's beat me to the spot. Her cheeks are bright pink, thanks to the wind that's blowing off the ocean today. Her hair whips around her face, making her freckles look like they're playing a game of peekaboo with me.

"Where you been, Chuck?" she asks, hopping from one high-top sneaker to the next. The sun glints off her head, and she's so shiny, I blink.

I shrug and start walking, hoping she'll change the subject.

"I overslept," I tell her nervously. Franki can sniff a lie on me a mile away.

To be honest, it's Lucy's fault I'm late. And the reason is so weird, I'm trying not to think about it.

I woke up to the sound of people yelling. Actually, my mom was yelling. Something else was whining. Like a dog.

At first, I tried covering my head with my pillow, but when I realized it wasn't going to stop, I sat up and pressed my ear to the wall so I could hear better.

"What's gotten into you today?" My mom's voice was muffled but clearly irritated. "Usually you are up and dressed by now."

More whining.

"Lucy," I heard her say, "I've got a double shift today. I don't have time for this sort of nonsense."

I tiptoed down the hall, wanting to check out the "nonsense" for myself. When I got to my sister's room and peeked around the corner, I wished I'd just stayed in bed.

My mom was standing next to my sister, holding out a purple skirt with bright-yellow butterflies on it and Lucy's trademark pink bow. Lucy sat on the floor, shaking her head. Her hair hung in a stringy mess, making her look more like a wild animal than my kid sister. When my mom tried to hand her the bow, she let out a whimper and started scratching behind her ear.

My heart skipped a beat as I thought back to what I'd written in my journal the night before.

Where the Imbecile had once been, there was now a dog.

"Lucille Evelyn Burger," my mother was saying, throwing the skirt on the bed. "I don't know what kind of game this is, but it's not amusing." She clipped the bow to the top of my sister's head and started toward the door. "You have five minutes to be dressed and downstairs or you'll be finding your own ride to school this morning."

I ran back to my room, sliding under the covers and pulling them up to my nose. Fifteen minutes later, I heard the crunch of my mom's tires backing out of the driveway. Sitting up, I peeked out the window. My sister sat in the backseat, her bow hanging sideways off her head and her tongue hanging halfway out of her mouth.

I grabbed my science journal, which was lying at the foot of my bed.

Goose bumps tickled my neck as I reread what I'd written. Lucy acting like a dog was just a weird coincidence, right? Or maybe it was a trick. Yeah, that was probably it. Lucy loves messing with my stuff. I bet she found my journal and thought it would be funny to pretend like she was a dog, just to freak me out.

Well, I'm not falling for it, I'd told myself. I threw on my clothes, then bolted down the stairs and out the door, too late to bother with breakfast.

Now, walking with Franki, I think about running all this by her, but she's already pressing me with questions of her own.

"And what about Saturday?" she says, an accusing look on her face. "I thought we were going to the beach."

I kick a small piece of granite off the sidewalk and into the street.

"I tried to call, but it wouldn't go through."

"Phone's off." She shrugs. "No one bothered to pay the bill."

I sneak a quick glance at her. "Everything okay?"

She rolls her eyes at me. "Stop trying to change the subject, Chuck. So, where were you anyway?"

She glares at me as we walk.

"I went to the mall," I mumble.

"The mall?" She laughs as if I made a joke. "Like, where they sell perfume and underwear?"

"Franki, can we talk about something else?"

She continues like she didn't hear me. "Why the mall?"

I sigh. "It was my mom's idea. She thinks I should put more effort into my appearance."

"Well . . ." she says.

"Well, what?"

She points to my shorts. "You've had those since fourth grade."

I look down. "They're comfortable."

She smiles. "At least she cares. Your mom, I mean."

"Caring is one thing. Making me wear a button-down shirt to the fall festival because she thinks that it's important to—"

"Festival?" She stops in the middle of the sidewalk.

Uh-oh. Now she's really going to let me have it.

"Since when did you decide to go to the festival?" she asks.

"Look, Frank." I put my hands out, surrender style. "Don't give me a hard time about this, okay? Stella's making me go. Says she needs to drum up more school spirit, and she expects me to be a supportive kid brother." I kick another piece of granite and start walking again. "It's no big deal."

Franki skips along beside me, swinging her arms wide. "But it is a big deal!" she says, her grin the size of a soccer field. She throws an arm around my shoulder, and my stomach flips sideways. "Now we have something to do on Friday." I sneak a look to see if she's being serious. Unfortunately, I think she is.

"You *want* to go?" Surely she's messing with me. "What would you want to do that for?"

"Why wouldn't I?" she challenges.

"Well, y-you know—" I stammer, not sure what to say. "There's going to be dancing there and people get dressed up and I just didn't think you liked—"

She gives me a look that I don't recognize. "Didn't think I liked what?"

I shrug. "I don't know. . . . Stuff like that. Girly stuff."

She crosses her arms across her faded yellow T-shirt. "Well, maybe I do. And besides, it beats the heck out of being at home with Carl. If I have to spend one more afternoon watching my stupid stepfather chug beers while watching game shows, I might go bonkers." My mom says Franki's stepdad has a deep love for Budweiser and unemployment checks. "Plus,

Chuck," she says, jabbing my shoulder, "it might actually be fun. It's our first middle-school event together!" She winks, then races toward the crosswalk. I hesitate for a second, then take off after her.

But the belt around my gut is so tight, I can't catch up. Franki and me at a school event? Where there might be dancing? *Slow* dancing?

I don't have a good feeling about this.

CHAPTER

7

THANKS TO MATH CLASS AND THE ORDER OF operations, by second period I've completely forgotten about Franki, the festival, and dancing.

After slogging through first period language arts and the correct use of adverbs, it's time for math, a subject I like almost as much as science. Both make way more sense to me than words.

But today's lesson stinks.

"The order of operations is kind of like a grammar book for mathematicians," Mrs. McElfresh, my math teacher, tries to explain. "Even though you may know what the different numbers and symbols mean in an equation, if you don't follow certain rules, your answer will be very different from the correct one."

I think about this for a minute. Rules, rules, and more rules. They seem to be everywhere now. Wear this, don't do that. Be different, but don't stand out. Mess up just a little bit, and the whole outcome will change. The older I get, the more rules there are. And if I forget one? Things just seem to get worse.

I leave math class feeling less in control than ever.

Unfortunately, that's when my real trouble begins.

"Charlie!" I look up from the water fountain and see Stella floating toward me. I hunch my shoulders and turn away, but she's zeroing in fast. I'm not sure why Miss Popularity feels the need to seek me out in the middle of the sixth-grade hallway, but here she is, singsonging my name so everyone can hear.

She stops in front of me, arms crossed.

"Oh . . . hi," I mumble, staring at a ketchup stain on my sneaker.

"Do you realize I've been calling your name all the way from . . . Oh, never mind. Listen—Dad just texted and said Pickles is coming for dinner tonight." She grins, and I do too. Pickles is my dad's mom and our favorite relative. "He wants you to come home right after school." She reaches out to smooth down my hair, but I swat her away. Two girls with thick blond ponytails slide past us, giggling. My face burns like someone just shoved a space heater in front of me and turned it on high.

"Charlie?"

"What?" I say too loudly, pulling at the collar of my T-shirt.

"Straight home after school," Stella says calmly. "You. Today." She talks to me like English is my second language.

I'm about to remind her that I have soccer practice when *whap!* Something smashes into the back of my head, causing my eyeballs to roll like they're inside a pinball machine. Next thing I know, the smell of feet and pizza grease rushes toward me as my face meets the floor. Something oozes out of my nose.

I listen for Stella to scream once she realizes I'm lying in a pool of my own brain matter. Instead, she sighs like someone just cut her in the lunch line.

"Jeez, Boomer. What did you do that for?"

Uh-oh. I stop worrying about my liquefied brains and realize I have a much bigger problem on my hands.

Lying in a pool of my own gore is like Disneyland compared to dealing with Boomer Bodbreath.

Stella leans over me, a long piece of hair dangling in my face.

"Charlie?" She reaches down and grabs me under my armpits. "Get up. You're making a scene."

Me? A scene? She pulls me up, and I feel relieved. I can stand. That's a good thing.

"Boomer," I hear her say, "you could've really hurt someone."

"Sorry, Stel." The guy sounds like he eats rocks for lunch. "We were just goofing around is all." He gives me a slap on the back, then spins me around to face him, poking a thick finger into my chest. "You got snot on your shirt, kid."

I stare at the bright-blue 44 on his football jersey.

Boomer Bodbreath, the Gatehouse Vikings' best defensive tackle.

Boomer Bodbreath, the Pantser.

Stella cocks her head to one side and studies the two meat-heads who stand next to him. Their jerseys sport the numbers 17 and 32.

"That isn't even yours," she says, pointing to the black-and-white soccer ball lying at my feet. It takes me a minute to realize it's the cause of my almost-decapitation. "You guys hate soccer. Where'd you get it?"

"From the short kid," Boomer says. "You know—nerdy guy with glasses, weird eyebrows."

Stella and I exchange a look. Grant.

"He gave it to you?" Stella asks.

Boomer smirks.

"I guess you could say that." The goons behind him giggle. "He can't really use it right now anyway."

I feel the belt start tightening again. "What's that supposed to mean?" Stella asks him. "What did you do to him, Boomer?"

Boomer crosses his arms, which are twice as thick as my thighs. "Tell you what, Stella," he says, winking. "Go to the festival with me on Friday, and I'll tell you where he is." The goons nod in unison. "Whaddya say?"

Stella picks up the ball with one hand and grabs my wrist with the other. She drags me behind her, past Boomer and his gang.

"Your loss!" Boomer calls out as I trip down the hall behind my sister.

It's not difficult to find Grant. He's inside the screaming locker.

"Help! Someone!" His voice is higher than normal, which is pretty impressive, considering he already sings soprano in the sixth-grade choir. "I think maybe I'm having a panic attack in here!"

It takes a few minutes before Stella can get Grant to calm down enough to tell her his locker combination. She pops the lever and he flops out, his bushy eyebrows and too-wide eyes making him look a little bit like Cookie Monster. "Oh, man . . . Oh, wow," he says, pulling down his shirt. I wrinkle my nose at the smell that follows him out.

"Jeez, Grant," I say, and try to breathe through my mouth. "What the . . ."

Stella gets right to business. "Okay, guys, let's go." She starts toward the front of the school but stops when she realizes we're not following her. "We need to find Dr. Moody. He'll want a full report, and Charlie and I will serve as your witnesses, Grant."

This would almost be funny if it weren't so ridiculous. If you're going to rat out a guy like Boomer Bodbreath, you better have your spot in the witness protection program all lined up. What planet is my sister living on anyway?

Nobody budges.

"Fine," she says, tossing Grant his soccer ball. "But don't say I didn't try to help you guys." She turns and stomps off, leaving us alone in the hallway.

I slam Grant's locker closed, then fiddle with the lock, not wanting to look him in the eye. "How'd you get mixed up with Boomer and his crew in the first place?"

He wipes his nose with his sleeve. "How should I know? One minute I'm juggling my ball in the hallway—and the next, this maniac is in my face, telling me to hand it over, or else. When I didn't, he said he'd make my decision easy. Next thing I know, I'm in my locker."

He adjusts his glasses. "Look, I need to go to the office, Charlie." He starts to push past me, but I grab his arm.

"What are you thinking, Grant?" He must be living on the same planet as my sister. "Are you nuts? Telling on Boomer is like a suicide mission. You really want to be on that maniac's radar?"

"Shut up, Burger," he hisses. "You have no idea what you're talking about."

"Listen." I put my arm around his shoulder. "We're measly

sixth graders. Our job is to lie low and not call attention to ourselves this year."

He pulls away from me and lifts the bottom of his shirt. A dark stain is spreading across the front of his khakis. "I'll tell you what I know, Burger. I know that if I don't call my mom and ask her to bring me some new pants, every single person at this crummy school is going to know I just got the pee scared right out of me. Think that's going to help me not call attention to myself?"

He shoves past me, and this time I let him go.

I drop my head in my hands. Boomer Bodbreath is one dangerous human being.

CHAPTER

I DECIDE TO TELL FRANKI ABOUT GRANT'S run-in with Boomer, but I leave out the pants-wetting part. Some stuff is just too personal to tell a girl, even if she is your best friend.

I should've known the whole thing would make her flaming mad.

"I told you, Chuck," she mumbles through a mouthful of veggie burger. Franki's on the free lunch plan at school, but she'd rather eat one of my dad's burgers any day. He always puts an extra one in my lunch box, just for her.

"Told me what?" I smash my milk container flat. I'm not in the mood for one of Franki's lectures today.

"That things would get worse," she says, waving her burger

in front of my face. "Take my stepfather, for instance. That man is a bona fide, card-carrying bully, and he'll keep doing what he wants until somebody stops him." She stabs at a soggy green bean with her fork but just moves it around on her tray. "Last night? He came home with four of his buddies and told Rose to clear the table so they could play a round of Texas Hold'em. When I reminded him that it was a school night, you know what he did?" She doesn't wait for my answer. "He told me to make myself useful and go round up some beers."

I take a small bite of my own burger, but I can't seem to swallow it. I wonder how Dude would handle a guy like Carl.

"And you know what Lila did?" I shake my head, but I can already guess the answer. Lila is Franki's mom and is pretty wimpy when it comes to Carl.

"She hustled me into the kitchen and begged me to be nice for once, saying it would make everyone's life much easier." Her eyes blaze. "Ha! That man's life couldn't *get* any easier if someone walked in and handed him a million bucks."

She stuffs the last of the burger into her mouth and chews with such force, I'm afraid she's going to break a tooth. Watching her, I think about the time my dad said that someday Franki is going to be quite the looker.

"Stop looking at me like that."

"Like what?" I say too quickly.

"I don't know, all . . . moony faced," she says, rolling her eyes at me. "All I'm saying, Chuck, is that kids like Boomer grow up to be guys like Carl." She picks up her tray. "And someone has to have the power to stop them."

And then she's gone and I can't stop wondering: *When did Franki Saylor turn into such a girl?*

CHAPTER

THAT AFTERNOON, I RUSH HOME FROM SOCCER
practice, knowing Pickles is already there. When I get to
our driveway, I see the beat-up yellow Volkswagen bug parked
sideways in our driveway, the two front wheels dangerously
close to my mom's flower garden. I smile and take the porch
steps two at a time.

"Pickles!" I shout.

Pickles isn't like most grandmas. She likes cigars and spends
a lot of time at comic book conventions. After my grandpa
died, she decided Boston was too far away from us and moved
to Salem, where she opened the biggest toy store on the North
Shore. From potato guns to penny candy to three-hundred-
piece Lego sets, you can find it all at Pickles's Place. Everything
great is in that store.

The last time I went was the Sunday before school started. Pickles had just gotten back from a toy convention in Baltimore and had asked my sisters and me to spend the day with her. Stella had cheerleading camp, but my mom said Lucy and I could go as long as we wore our seat belts, and Pickles promised to have us home before dark.

She picked us up in the Volkswagen, and we headed down Route 128, sharing her bubble gum stash from the glove compartment and singing old show tunes from *South Pacific*. When we got to her store, she flung her arms wide and announced, "Go crazy, kiddos!" then disappeared into her back office. The next two hours were ours.

I started where I always did: the candy wall. Rows of large glass jars held everything from lemon drops to mini chocolate bars. I tried every single flavor of jelly bean until I couldn't stomach anymore. After a while, I plugged a few dimes into the player piano, and we sang along to "The Yellow Rose of Texas" while Lucy redesigned the train track running across the floor and I test-drove the pogo sticks that had just been delivered. We sang at the tip-top of our lungs, because no one was there to say we couldn't.

At twelve o'clock sharp Pickles reappeared, ready for lunch at the diner next door.

Two hours later my belly was full of ham on rye, Lucy was stuffed with egg salad, and both of our arms were full of loot.

Pickles had to drive over the speed limit most of the way, but she got us home by dusk. My dad came out to help us carry in our packages, but my mom stayed in the doorway.

"You're spoiling those kids, Pickles," she warned, but she smiled a little while she said it.

"It's my job," Pickles replied, pointing her unlit cigar out the window. "I'm the grandma."

My dad laughed. "Don't be a stranger," he told her.

"There are no strangers here—only friends you haven't yet met," she said, which is how she always responds. Then she winked. "That's a quote by Yeats, kiddos. Look him up."

And with that, she was gone.

But that was all before middle school started, and I haven't seen her until now.

■ ■ ■

I find her in the kitchen with my dad. They stop talking as soon as I walk in.

"Well, well." She grins. "Look what the cat dragged in."

She sets down the onion she was slicing and walks over to me. I notice that her long white hair has strands of purple running through it. Last time I saw her, they were orange.

Stella thinks Pickles moved to Salem because she's a witch. My mom says that's ridiculous, but sometimes I like to pretend it's true.

"Charlie," she says, putting both hands on my cheeks, rubbing them as if to make sure I'm real. "You are a pleasant sight for this old woman's eyes."

"What are you doing here?" I ask her.

She pretends to look hurt. "Now, what kind of a question is that for your grandmother?"

"It's just—well, it's a weeknight. You usually come on Sundays."

"Your father called and said he was making eggplant parmesan. He knows it's one of my favorites." She grins. "Plus," she says, crossing her arms, "my only grandson just started middle school last week. Those are both good reasons for a visit, don't you think?"

"Sure," I say, though I can't imagine going anywhere for eggplant parmesan.

She motions for me to sit down, then does the same. Leaning her elbows on the table, she searches my face like it's a road map. "So, tell me all about sixth grade."

I shrug. "There's not much to tell."

"Think of something."

I pick at a scab on my elbow. "My science teacher wears cowboy hats and says 'pardner' a lot. He's sort of weird."

She raises her eyebrows. "Science, huh?"

I nod. "He gave us these journals, but told us to write stories in them instead of science stuff."

She looks over her shoulder at my dad, then back at me. "Have you written anything yet?"

"Kind of," I tell her, not sure I want to talk about this. Writing make-believe stories about a superhero in my sixth-grade science journal is a little awkward. But telling my grandmother about it is even worse.

Lucky for me, my mom and Stella walk in. They're fighting. About shoes.

"It's not that I *want* them, Mom. I *need* them. There's a difference."

My mom unbuckles her police belt and lays it on the bench next to the back door. "Just because Stacey Stalen's mother bought her new shoes to go with the new uniforms doesn't mean I have to."

"But it's not just Stacey, Mom. Lori Crabtree's mother bought them for her, and so did Betsy Hamilton's, even though her dad just got laid off. Do you know how this is going to look? I mean, I'm the captain!"

My mom bites her thumb. "Money doesn't grow on trees, Stella."

"I know that." Stella rolls her eyes like this is the most obvious thing in the world. "But what you don't realize—"

Pickles stands and walks over to my sister. "What you don't realize, Stella dear, is that your mother's working hard to keep you in the shoes you have on your feet right now." Stella looks down. "Now," she continues, "if you'd like to earn some money to buy those new shoes yourself, I've got a big shipment coming into the toy store two weeks from Saturday." She glances over at my mom. "If it's okay with your parents, you could come help me sort and organize it before the afternoon crowd shows up."

"Sounds fine by me," my mom says as my dad raises his spatula in agreement.

Stella throws her arms around Pickles's neck.

"Oh my gosh, Pickles, really? That would be great!"

"Good." She turns to me. "You come too, if you want."

I nod, but I doubt I'll go. I love spending time with Pickles, but after last week's mall trip, the idea of another Saturday inside any store makes me feel squirmy, even if it is the best toy store on the planet.

After dinner, I'm loading the dishwasher when Pickles comes into the kitchen. She grabs a dish towel and begins to dry the casserole dish. Her hands shake a little.

"So, other than this science teacher, do you like it? Middle school, I mean."

I think about my run-in with Boomer, and Grant getting stuffed into his locker. I think about the order of operations and how if you don't follow certain rules, the answers will be all wrong. And I think about Franki and the fall festival and how Stella said middle school was going to change everything between us.

"I don't know," I say, turning on the faucet. "Everything seemed a lot less complicated before."

She sets the dish down. "You know, you remind me a lot of your grandpa." She taps the side of her head. "You got his smarts. His eyes, too."

"What was he like, Pickles?" I ask. "No one talks about him much."

She stares out the window into the backyard. "He was one of the good guys. Kind, curious, brave . . ." She smiles, but her face looks sad. "They don't make many like him anymore. Not many at all."

"What happened to him, Pickles?" I ask.

"It was an accident."

"In his lab? Was he working on a new invention?"

"The details aren't really important, Charlie, but this part is." She turns and looks at me. "He would have been very proud of you and the person you're becoming."

I look down at the suds in the sink. "Too bad I don't have a clue who that person is."

"You don't have to right now. Let your imagination be in charge of that for a while."

A prickly feeling plays at the back of my neck, and suddenly the kitchen feels too hot. I pull at the collar of my T-shirt.

"You okay?" she asks.

"Yeah," I say. "It's just that Mr. P said something like that when he gave us the journals."

"The science teacher?"

"Yeah. He told us we should let our imaginations run like a pack of wild ponies."

She laughs. "Sounds familiar."

"What do you mean?"

"Your grandfather always said that until people understand the importance of their imaginations, they have nothing to offer the world of science." She wags a finger at me. "Just remember, Charlie. Things aren't always what they seem. And the answers aren't as obvious as you think."

"What answers?" I say, confused. "I don't even know the questions."

She taps her head again. "You're a smart cookie. You'll think of some good ones. I'm sure of it."

■ ■ ■

That night, after Pickles leaves, I'm heading to my room when I hear a chewing noise coming from Lucy's. I tell myself to ignore it, to keep walking, but I can't help myself. I peek around the corner.

"Lucy!" She looks up at me from where she's lying in the middle of her rug. "Is that . . . Are you . . . ?"

One of my soccer cleats sits on the floor next to her. I walk in and pick it up. The top of it is soaking wet.

"Have you been chewing on this?" I demand. She lets out a whimper.

I'm about to yell for my mom, but change my mind. Instead I shove the shoe in her face.

"Stay out of my room and away from my stuff, do you hear me?" I wave it under her nose. "Or next time, you're going to get it."

A low growl comes from somewhere deep inside her. I bolt out the door, holding the slobbery shoe in front of me.

When I get to my room, I slam the door and lean against it. My head is swimming as I start looking around for my other cleat. And that's when I see it.

A plain orange envelope leans against my computer screen.

I slide my finger under the flap and pull out a single piece of paper. Right away, I recognize Pickles's handwriting:

WORDS CAN BE POWERFUL.
BELIEVE IN THEIR MAGIC AND ANYTHING CAN HAPPEN.

I sit down. It's the same thing Mr. P said when he handed me my journal. Pickles didn't come here tonight just for my dad's eggplant parmesan or to grill me about middle school. My grandmother and my science teacher are both trying to tell me something, but what?

I reach down and open my backpack. As soon as my fingers touch the journal, the now-familiar shock runs from my fingertips up the inside of my arm. I stare at the journal for a minute, thinking about experiments and words and magic. I think about what happened today with Boomer, and what Franki said about kids like him growing up to be guys like her stepdad.

Unless, maybe, someone has the power to stop them.

I open my journal and start writing.

September 14
Episode 3: The Big Blowup

The space monster advanced quickly, his suit of armor clanging against the rocky ground. His mouth was pulled wide in an evil grin, revealing two rows of razor-sharp teeth and a barbed tongue. He was three times the size of any creature on Planet Splodii and a bazillion times more powerful.

His mission? Ingest a superhero for lunch, then claim galactic domination by dinnertime.

The menacing creature's name was Bloogfer, and he had a secret weapon that no other being in the universe possessed: Bodyodor Blowout. He could let off a smell that would invade victims' bodies through their nostrils, mouths, and ear canals, an odor so grotesque, their eyes would water uncontrollably, their bodies would be thrown into bone-shattering convulsions, and their mouths would fill with a taste so disgusting that no amount of spitting or even upchucking could get rid of it. It was a superpower that had served him well on his rampage of slaughter throughout the universe.

Until today.

As Bloogfer prepared to unleash his killer stink upon Planet Splodii, Dude and his new dog, Bill, appeared on the horizon. Closing his eyes, Dude called upon Superpower #34: Biological Manipulation. As Bloogfer's smell crept across the planet, everyone began to cough and writhe on the ground. Luckily, Dude's ability to control his urge to react kept him protected. He stood his ground. The monster stopped for a moment, shaking his head.

"You don't belong here, Bloogfer," Dude growled. "Time for you to crawl back into your underground hole before I do something we'll both regret."

The evil grin reappeared on the monster's face. He loved a good challenge. Taking a quick whiff of his armpit for reinforcement, he clanged toward Dude, the sound of metal grinding on metal, causing Dude's sensitive ears to burn. As he reached to cover them, the monster lunged, his arms as thick as tree trunks.

Squeezing his eyes closed, Dude called on Superpower #45: Inhuman Reflexes. He ducked, easily avoiding the potentially fatal blow.

"Come on, you big oaf," Dude teased. "Can't you do better than that?"

Bloogfer raged. Again, he hurled himself toward Dude, his eyes blazing, his lips curled. Dude waited—then gracefully slid to the left, causing the raging monster to fly past and crash head-on into a stone wall behind him. As he roared in frustration, Dude grinned, enjoying this more than he had thought he would.

"You know what, Bloog?" Dude said, eyeing the mass of metal lying on the ground. "Your antics bore me. I've had enough for today." Extending his right arm, he aimed at the creature's metal-plated chest, squeezed his eyes shut, and waited. It was time for him to call on his shape-shifting powers and transform his arm into his most secret weapon—the Exterminizer.

Zap! His fingers quivered for less than a nanosecond before the blast shot out of him, straight toward his target's chest. The sizzling sound reminded him of bacon grease, and the snapping and popping as the electricity zipped through the air made his stomach growl with memories of that morning's breakfast. The jolt collided with Bloogfer's armor, and the sound was spectacular, the Exterminizer's power smashing into the metal armor. A stream of fireworks began to zip and zing off Bloogfer's chest, making him shimmy uncontrollably across the rocky surface. Within seconds, the show was over, and as the last of the sparks died out, the crowd that had gathered to watch the spectacle began to clap wildly, hooting and whistling for their leader who had—as always—once again saved the day.

Bloogfer lay still, glancing down at his now-exposed flesh. He let out a small whimper when he saw the shiny pink skin where only moments before his steel-plated armor had been.

"What have you done, Explodius? You have stripped me of my protective shields!"

"Yes, Bloogfer." Dude nodded. "And your powers, as well. No longer will you be a threat to even the weakest of creatures. But I have spared your life, and for that you should thank me."

Dude aimed again, and with one last blast, shot the monster off Planet Splodii and into the atmosphere beyond.

"But," he called out as the pink blob grew smaller and smaller in the distance, "should you ever return, rest assured you will not live to see another day!"

CHAPTER 10

IT'S FRIDAY AFTERNOON, AND I'M SLUMPED in the corner of the hallway, next to the gym, waiting on Franki. It's the day that I've been dreading all week—the fall festival. Just thinking the words makes me cringe.

After the pantsing incident and my hallway face-plant, I've managed to stay out of the limelight. Too bad I can't say the same for everybody.

On Wednesday, Bennett Kraus left school with a bloody nose after someone tied his shoelaces together in French class and he tripped over Ms. DuCharme's seven-foot replica of the Eiffel Tower. Dr. Moody said Bennett was fine, but he hasn't been back all week.

On Thursday, Allen Foxworthy went home in tears after getting stuck in the boys' bathroom for three hours straight.

Literally. Someone decided it would be funny to drip Krazy Glue all over the toilet seats, and it took two teachers, the school nurse, and Dr. Moody to get him unstuck.

Allen hasn't been back, either.

Even though every kid at Gatehouse knows that Boomer Bodbreath is behind these pranks, no one can prove it. So far he's gotten off scot-free.

I reach into my backpack and pull out my journal. Opening it up, I reread the last entry I wrote, the one about Bloogfer, and how Dude blew apart his armor and threatened to do worse if he showed up on Planet Splodii again. Flipping to the back of the notebook, I pull out Pickles's note, reading it for the billionth time.

WORDS CAN BE POWERFUL.
BELIEVE IN THEIR MAGIC AND ANYTHING CAN HAPPEN.

"Hey, Chuck."

I look up from my journal and grin. My mom says that Franki has the voice of a two-pack-a-day smoker, though I know for a fact she's never touched a cigarette in her life.

"That a love letter?" she says, pointing to the piece of paper. I scramble to my feet, stuffing it into my back pocket.

"Very funny," I say, forcing out a laugh. I stop when I see her face.

Something's different. Her hair is pulled back, and her eyelashes seem to have grown a mile overnight. She's got something glittery on her eyelids, and her normal T-shirt has been replaced with a lacy tank top.

"You got fruit punch on your mouth," I tell her, pointing to the red stain across her lips.

"It's lipstick," she says.

"Lipstick?"

"You say it like it's a bad word." Franki snorts. She punches my arm. "Don't be such a goob."

She smells different, too, like the girls who hang out at the mall. I can't quit staring at her.

"Close your mouth, Charlie," she says, then reaches into her backpack. "Wait till you see what I got!" She pulls her hand out and produces two king-size candy bars. "There's a ton of free food down the eighth-grade hallway," she says, handing me one. "I've already had a hot dog and three chocolate doughnuts. With sprinkles."

I rip open the candy wrapper with my teeth. This is more like Franki.

The double doors behind us swing open, and the heavy beat of a popular pop song blasts out. Two girls from Stella's cheer team walk past us, giggling.

I lean close to Franki's ear so she can hear me above the music. "Hey, Frank," I say, trying not to take a deep whiff of her. "Let's get out of here. We'll grab our pails from my house and head to the cove. It's perfect clamming weather and you can borrow a sweatshirt and—"

She stares at me like I've suggested we rob a bank. "What's wrong with you, Chuck? We're at our first middle-school festival. We're supposed to be meeting people, hanging out, having fun. Come on, let's go in and check out the dance."

She grabs my hand, and I'm too shocked to say no.

She pulls the gym door open, and we enter a whole different world. Bright-white lights strobe on and off, making me feel queasy. The music pulses through my veins, the beat pushes up through my feet, and suddenly my whole body is vibrating. I squint but can't make out anything but a dark mass of bodies in the center of the room. The smell of sweat and bubble gum mix together and make me want to sneeze. Franki yanks me toward the center of the gym floor.

Bodies surround us, bump up against us. The air is thick, like the time my parents took us to Florida for spring break. I feel like I'm breathing through a straw.

"Dance, Chuck, dance!" Franki squeezes my arms and lets out an unrecognizable giggle, jerking and jolting against me like she's having a seizure. She bumps her hip against mine, shoving me off-balance, and I slam into the girl next to me. My armpits are so sticky, I wish I'd listened to Stella when she suggested I wear deodorant.

The girl glares at me like I'm radioactive.

I start looking around for the closest escape route when the music stops and the gym explodes in light.

Franki blinks. She cocks her head to one side, listening as the DJ announces a fifteen-minute break. People start to shuffle toward the bathroom and the food.

"Wow . . . uh . . . okay," I say, running my fingers through my hair. "That was great. So . . ." I say, hooking my finger toward the door, "you ready to go?" I raise my eyebrows, hopeful.

Franki crosses her arms, grinning. "Oh, come on. Wasn't that kind of fun?"

Fun like a lobotomy. I try to think of something, quick. If I don't get out now, I'm doomed.

"How about another hot dog? Or snow cone?" I start toward the door, then peek over my shoulder. She's not budging.

"Franki . . ." My voice sounds whiny, but I'm desperate.

She lifts her chin and turns away from me. "I want to dance."

I look around. Kids are starting to wander back in, shoving the last bites of hot dog or greasy pizza into their mouths. "Frank," I whisper, "this is kind of embarrassing."

"Embarrassing?" she says. She leans away from me, her hands on her hips. "Well, gosh, I certainly wouldn't want to do anything to *embarrass* you."

Then right there in the middle of the school gym, she reaches out and throws her arms around my neck.

"Ack! Get off!" I try to break free, but it's no use. The girl may be scrawny, but boy, is she strong.

"I swear, Charlie Burger, you are such a—"

She drops her arms, staring at something behind me. Every hair on my body starts to sizzle.

I turn, even though I know I shouldn't. As soon as I see him, my insides drop into my sneakers.

Boomer Bodbreath and his baboons are beelining it straight for Franki and me.

CHAPTER
11

"WHAT'S HAPPENING, BABIES?" THE FLUORESCENT lighting inside the gym gives Boomer's skin a strange yellow tint, and his eyes look more sadistic than ever. "Is someone not sharing over here?"

He moves between us, the 44 on his football jersey filling my vision.

He looks Franki up and down in a way that makes me think about the stray dogs that hang around outside Drozdov's butcher shop, waiting for a piece of scrap meat.

"Maybe you're not all babies," he says, and the two goons behind him snicker.

I clear my throat. "Nothing's happening, Boomer." If I'd just stuffed my mouth with dirt, it would feel less dry. "In fact, we were kind of on our way out. It's getting late, and my dad's probably waiting for us. . . ." I stop when Boomer's meaty hand palms my forehead.

"Looks like a lovers' spat to me." His eyes search my face, like he's trying to figure out what to do with me. I keep my own eyes glued to the blue 44 like it's the most important thing in the room. He drops his palm onto my shoulder. "Though, I think you might be out of your league with this one."

I gulp.

"I asked you a question."

Technically, that was a statement and not a question, I want to say, but instead I nod.

"Uh, sure, Boomer," I tell him. "You're absolutely right."

He bends in closer.

"About which part?"

"Huh?" I'm starting to feel dizzy.

Franki steps in between us. "Why don't you leave us alone?" She crinkles her nose. "And take that smell with you."

This is not going to end well, I think.

Boomer digs his fingers deeper into my shoulder, and I wince.

"Your girlfriend is not very nice," he says. "Someone needs to teach her some manners."

I start to say something, but Franki cuts me off.

"You don't scare us," she says, the fists at her sides telling me she's past mad. "Now get out of here so the rest of us can dance."

A crowd has started to gather around.

Boomer tries to laugh, but it comes out more like a snort.

"You call that dancing?" His eyes scan the group. "I don't know about the rest of you, but I've never seen dancing like that before." A few kids snort back in agreement.

"Oh, come on, Boomer," Franki says. "You've been at Gatehouse for how many years? Four? Five? Guess you flunked dancing, too."

The room goes silent.

"If you weren't such an idiot," she says, her voice ice-cold, "I'd almost feel sorry for you."

Boomer moves so quickly, I don't see it coming. In less than a nanosecond, he's grabbed a chunk of Franki's hair and twisted it into his fist, pulling her so close that her freckly face is pressed right up against his. His lips are against her earlobe, and the only sound is someone's heartbeat pounding in my ear.

I have to do something, I think, but shake the thought from my head. This is Franki. She knows how to take care of herself. Any second and she's going to make Boomer Bodbreath wish he'd never met her.

But Boomer keeps whispering something in her ear, something that makes Franki just stand there like she's paralyzed. She doesn't argue, or even try to get away. It's like his words have zapped the fight right out of her.

I close my eyes, and goose bumps sizzle across my skin.

You're not a superhero, I tell myself. *You don't have the power to do anything about this.*

Or do I?

CHAPTER

12

I SQUEEZE MY EYES CLOSED AND THINK about what I wrote about Bloogfer. Dude's face fills the darkness behind my eyeballs, and a billion prickly electrons jump to life inside me. They pulse through my veins, bouncing around like they're on a sugar high.

Without thinking, I reach out my hand and point it in Boomer's direction. My arm shimmies and shakes like my dad's did two weeks ago when he shocked himself trying to rewire his juice machine.

And then—as quickly as it started—it's over. I open my eyes. The image of Dude is gone.

And so is Franki.

I scan the crowd but can't see her anywhere. The room has gone crazy; people are pushing and shoving me aside, jockeying for a spot around something I can't see. I crane my neck, but an elbow in my face prevents me from getting a good look.

"Get a load of that!" I hear.

"Wow . . ." Someone whistles.

"What's he thinking? Why would he do that in here?"

I stand on my tiptoes, trying to see over the mob of heads, but it's no use. Everyone's angling for a front-row view. Finally, I see an opening in the bodies and duck down, squeezing my way to the front of the pack.

And there—center stage, stands Boomer.

Naked.

Birthday suit naked.

I think about my journal and what I wrote.

Bloogfer lay still, glancing down at his now-exposed flesh.

Did I make this happen?

The crowd explodes. Plastic cups, half-eaten hot dog buns, and candy wrappers hurl past me as people scream, whistle, and stomp the floor. Boomer just stands there, staring down at himself like he's waiting for someone to tell him the punch line. Now *I* almost feel sorry for him.

A brick-shaped kid sporting a bright-blue 32 across his jersey pushes through the crowd. He scoops Boomer's pile of clothes off the floor and shoves it at his chest. Boomer just stares, like he's never seen his clothes before. The crowd roars. The kid next to me is laughing so hard, tears roll down his cheeks.

The double doors fly open, and Dr. Moody marches in, followed by Mr. P and a janitor.

"Enough!" Dr. Moody's voice booms across the gym and hits us like a bucket of cold water. Everyone freezes. He crosses the room and grabs Boomer's arm, pulling him toward the exit and signaling for Number 32 to follow. As they head out, Boomer flashes a full-on shot of his bare backside, which brings the crowd roaring back to life, until Mr. P sticks two fingers in his mouth and lets out a whistle that shuts everyone up for good.

He tilts his cowboy hat back and surveys the crowd. "Well, I reckon someone best start explaining." His blue eyes darken like they did before, a storm cloud moving across them.

No one moves.

"Don't make me say it twice."

Dolores Bryant speaks up first.

"It was wild, Mr. P," she says breathlessly. She holds her right hand in her left, as if she's afraid it will fall off if she doesn't. "We had just come back from the refreshment table, and for some reason Boomer Bodbreath had stripped in front of the entire room." She smoothes her blouse and plays with the tiny round buttons that march down the front. "It was very inappropriate. But don't worry, I'll be making a full report to the student council next week."

"I'm sure you will, Dolores." Mr. P scans the room, and his eyes come to rest on mine. I look away, fast.

"Y'all need to get busy straightening this mess up," he says, raising his hand before anyone can protest. "And I don't want to hear no bellyaching about it. Party's over."

I want to look for Franki but don't want to call any attention to myself. Instead, I start picking up plastic cups and keeping an eye out for her bright-green high-tops.

"Charlie." I look up. Mr. P stands over me, holding something in his hands.

My science journal.

He nods at me. "Has your name on it, so I reckon it's yours." I grab it, and goose bumps crackle at the base of my neck.

I try to keep my voice from shaking. "Where did you find it?"

"I didn't find it," he says, and the thundercloud in his eyes shifts a little. "It found you."

"Oh. Well, thanks."

For a split second I think I see a spark of blue—as shiny as a piece of sea glass—wink at me through the gray. "It's a special journal, pardner," he says. "Best not let it out of your sight again. You never know when it might come in handy."

He turns on his boot heel and glides across the gym floor. I'm pretty sure he's whistling one of Pickles's favorite show tunes when Dolores rushes up to him, blabbering away about what to do with the leftover hot dogs and did he know that there's a toilet overflowing in the girls' bathroom?

I look down at the journal. My whole right arm begins to tingle.

■ ■ ■

Twenty minutes later, I still haven't found Franki, but Stella's found me. Grabbing my shirtsleeve, she hauls me toward the front doors.

"I've been looking for you everywhere," she says, blowing a strand of hair out of her face. "Dad texted and said he's going to be here any minute, and he's got a van full of veggie burgers that need to be dropped off before dinner."

I have to practically run to keep up with her.

"But I've got to find—"

"Come *on*, Charlie."

We get to the main entrance, and Stella pushes the double doors open. The air is heavy with the smell of salt and seaweed. I scan the crowd of kids waiting for their rides to show up. Still no Franki.

I hear a quick honk as the old blue van pulls around the corner, my dad's arm waving out the window.

"Hey, guys," he calls out. "How was the—" He stops when he sees me. "What's wrong with *you*? You look like you've seen a ghost."

Stella jumps into the front seat, waving at a few of her friends. I slide into the back as my dad turns to get a better look at me.

"Everything okay?"

I nod, staring out the window.

"Oh, don't worry about him, Dad," Stella says, answering for me. "The first school festival can be a bit . . . overwhelming for a sixth grader."

CHAPTER

13

I WAKE UP IN THE MIDDLE OF THE NIGHT, MY room so black, I can't tell if my eyelids are open or closed.

I toss and turn, but all I can think about is the journal.

Finally, I can't stand it anymore. I kick off the blankets and climb out of bed. The floorboards creak as I tiptoe across the room and flip on my desk lamp.

It sits smack-dab in the middle of a pile of papers, the soft leather cover practically glowing under the warm light.

As soon as I touch it, the prickling starts. It zips through my fingers and up the inside of my arm.

Calm down, I tell myself. *This isn't what you think.* Stuff like this only happens in Hollywood movies and science-fiction books.

I flip to the last entry, the one I wrote about Bloogfer.

I squint at the words, but all I can think about are the ones Mr. P said to me in the gym.

I didn't find it. . . . It found you.

I flip back another page and try to read the one about the Imbecile, but again, it's no use. Mr. P's voice is still in my head.

It's a special journal, pardner.

Tiptoeing into the hallway, I peek around the corner and into Lucy's room. The pink polka-dotted night-light gives the room a rose-colored glow. Her stuffed animals are lined up across her bed, standing guard, like usual.

Only Lucy isn't in the bed.

I look down. There, in the middle of the rug, my sister sleeps curled up in a ball. Her leg twitches, like she's chasing something in her sleep.

I hurry back to my room. The magnolia tree outside my window sways in the wind, its branches tap-tapping on my windowsill. I grab my jeans off the floor and dig into the back pocket, finding Pickles's note again.

WORDS CAN BE POWERFUL.
BELIEVE IN THEIR MAGIC AND ANYTHING CAN HAPPEN.

Pickles said the answers wouldn't be as obvious as they seem. But I think I know someone who can at least help me start figuring out the questions.

CHAPTER
14

MONDAY MORNING, I HIGHTAIL IT TO SCHOOL before anyone's awake. The sun is just starting to peek above Gatehouse as I run across the street and then the courtyard. I take the steps two at a time and try the double doors, but they are still locked. Even the janitors aren't here yet.

I lean against the cold brick wall and watch the colors in the sky change as the sun climbs higher. A lonesome seagull cries out overhead, probably feeling ripped off now that all the tourists have left.

I stuff my hands into my pockets and exhale, my breath coming out in puffs. Normally, I would never be at school this early, but I've got to talk to Mr. P before first period. Maybe he can help me figure out if there's some connection between the things I'm writing in my journal and the things that are happening around me.

Ten minutes later, I can't feel my toes, and I'm starting to think this wasn't such a great idea, when suddenly the front door bangs open and the rim of a dark gray cowboy hat pokes out.

"Mornin'," a deep voice behind the door says. "You looking for me, pardner?"

I glance across the parking lot. Not a car in sight.

What did he do, sleep at the school?

He sticks an arm out, motioning me toward him.

"You coming in? It's colder than witch's snot out there."

He pushes the door open wider, and I hesitate for just a millisecond before I push off the wall and walk toward him, ducking under his arm.

We walk past the office, still dark.

"I'm sorry to bug you so early, Mr. P, but I need to ask you—"

"Whoa, there," he says, cutting me off. "Let's hold those horses until we get to the lab."

I follow him down the sixth-grade hall. Our footsteps echo off the walls, and the emptiness makes me feel uneasy. I practically jump out of my skin when I hear a low groan and feel a vibration under my feet.

"Furnace starting up," says Mr. P. "Thing's older than me."

I let out my breath, not realizing I'd been holding it.

He stops in front of the science lab and pulls the door open. "All right, Charlie," he says, gesturing for me to go in first. "Let's get down to business."

I step into the room and look around. It's like I've entered a different world. A soft glow blankets the classroom, and the air is like a down jacket, warming me from the outside in. Strange music—jazz, I think—plays from an old turntable in the corner, and the smell of bacon—yes, bacon!—fills my nose, making my stomach rumble. An oversize leather chair takes up an entire corner of the room, and stacked next to it are books—towers of books—their bindings torn and the titles so worn, I can't make out what they say. A strange rug covers the floor, and no joke, I'm pretty sure it's a genuine cowhide.

"I reckon you could use a cup of joe this morning." Mr. P holds up a blue coffeepot, and I notice the small cookstove sitting on top of his desk. I shrug, as if drinking coffee with my teacher in a room that looks more like his house than a sixth-grade science lab is the most normal thing in the world.

He pours two cups, then hands one to me. I take a sip and spew it all over the wall. Brown spit drips from the periodic table in front of me.

"Ugh." I gag, scraping at my tongue with my fingers. "What *is* that?"

"Cowboy coffee," he says, taking a long swig. "Puts hair on your chest."

I keep scraping, though I'm pretty sure permanent damage has been done to my taste buds.

"Why don't you take a load off," he says. He settles in behind his desk, leaning back and plunking his boots on top of it.

I sit down in the leather chair across from him. When I scoot all the way back, my feet don't touch the floor.

"Mr. P," I say, "I need to ask you about the journal you gave me."

He picks up a strip of bacon and nods for me to go on.

"Remember when you first handed them out? You told us to write some junk down and—"

"Hold up a minute," he says, pointing the bacon at me. "I never said anything about writing 'junk.' Try again."

I think for a minute. "You said everyone has a story to tell."

"Go on."

"But that's the thing," I say. "I don't have any stories. So I made one up."

"And?"

"And now . . ." I trail off, not sure how to describe it.

"And now what?" He swings his boots off the desk and leans toward me. His eyes are clear blue now, not a hint of the

93

stormy gray from before. "What happened after you wrote this made-up story of yours?"

"That's the thing—I don't know, exactly." My throat feels tight, like someone's squeezing it. "It's like, somehow . . . these things I'm writing . . . It's almost like they're coming true."

"And?"

"And that's why I'm here. I was hoping you could help me make sense of it."

He takes another swig of coffee. "Remember what I told you, Charlie. A true scientist will ask questions about the things that don't make sense, not the things that do." He takes a bite of bacon.

"Well, this definitely doesn't make sense," I tell him.

He looks at me carefully. "Then I reckon it's time you start asking some questions."

I close my eyes, thinking. "On the first day of class, you asked me if I believed in magic." My scalp starts to tingle as I move forward in the chair. "Is that it, Mr. P? Is my science journal magical?"

He doesn't answer right away. When he finally does, his voice is deeper than before. "No, Charlie," he says. "The journal is not magical."

I flop backward, throwing my arm over my eyes. Of course the journal's not magical. It's just a stupid notebook.

I sit up and climb out of the chair. I'm ready to leave, to walk out the door and forget about all this, but a tight ball of heat starts to burn in my stomach. I turn back to him. "So, you're going to sit there and tell me that my sister acting like a dog and Boomer stripping naked—these things have nothing to do with the adventures I've been writing in my journal?"

"I'm not telling you that."

This guy is really starting to get on my nerves.

"Mr. P, no offense, but this whole thing is kind of—"

"Charlie, do you know what a catalyst is?"

Oh, great. *Now* he's going give me a science lesson?

"I don't think we've covered that yet," I mutter.

He continues. "A catalyst is a substance that increases the rate of a chemical reaction without itself suffering any permanent chemical change."

"I'm not really following," I say.

He stands up and walks in front of his desk. "A catalyst doesn't make something happen, Charlie." His eyes twinkle. "It only helps move it along. That journal may be serving as a catalyst between you and what you can do."

I narrow my eyes at him. "What do you mean, what I can do?"

"That's a question only you can answer. My job is to observe what's happening. Yours is to figure it out."

What a nutwad.

I grab my backpack off the floor.

"I have to go now, Mr. P," I tell him. "I just realized I forgot my math homework, and Mrs. McElfresh gets kind of irritated if—"

"I think you have a gift, Charlie. That journal is just serving as a way for you to get it out."

The ball of heat spreads. Whatever this is, it's one mean trick, that's for sure.

"Okay," I say, throwing my hands up in the air. "What if I wrote a story about a kid who wants a pony? Is one going to turn up in my front yard?" I take a step toward him. "And how about Dolores Bryant? Are we going to wake up and find out that some know-it-all sixth grader is now president of the United States, just because of something *she* writes?" My voice is starting to shake, but I don't care.

He pulls a toothpick out of his shirt pocket and points it at me. "It's not about the journal, Charlie. It's about you." He looks around, then bends closer to me. "I think you may be a bully buster."

I blink. "A bully what?"

"A bully buster. It's a special person, someone who possesses the power to make people see things in a way they haven't before. They are able to use that power to change things, hopefully for the better."

I scratch my head. "I don't know, Mr. P. I can barely remember to change my underwear."

He chuckles. "It's okay to have doubts, Charlie. If you didn't, it wouldn't count as an experiment, would it?"

As if on cue, the phone on his desk starts ringing. He strides over and lifts the receiver.

I watch as he nods a couple of times, mutters something, then hangs up. When he turns back around, his face seems more serious than before.

"I've got to deal with something, pardner," he says. He puts his hand on my shoulder. "Probably best you mosey on out of here now."

"One last question," I say.

He nods. "Shoot."

"Why me? I mean, I'm just some kid trying to make it through sixth grade alive. What makes you think I have what it takes to be a bully buster?"

"There are some theories, but—"

"But what?"

He looks over my head at the clock behind me.

"This gift . . . It may be passed down through families, kind of like red hair or dimples." He steers me toward the door. "But that's not the important part."

"Then what is?"

He gives me a gentle push into the hallway. "That you don't let that doubt I was talking about suffocate your imagination." He winks. "Remember—there is no rubric for this assignment."

He pulls the door shut before I can respond.

I look around. The hallway is starting to fill up around

me, and I hear Grant call my name from the other end. I push my face up against Mr. P's door for one last peek.

Through the narrow window I can see him. He's back at his desk, the phone receiver in his hand. And then I see something else.

The leather chair, turntable, and tower of books are all gone.

So is the coffeepot.

Even the smell of bacon has vanished.

I turn and bolt toward my locker, goose bumps tap dancing across my skin.

CHAPTER 15

FOR THE FIRST PART OF THE MORNING, I HAVE
a hard time focusing. I can't stop thinking about everything
Mr. P. said, about power and catalysts and gifts. By lunchtime
my head is spinning, and I've completely lost my appetite.

I peek into the cafeteria, but Franki's seat is empty. I wonder if she's mad at me for not walking with her to school this
morning. I tried to call, to tell her I had an early morning
project to work on, but her phone was still disconnected.

I'm thinking about heading to the library, when I hear
someone call my name.

"Charlie!" Stella waves at me from the front of the lunch
line, surrounded by a group of giggling girls. "Over here!"

Great, I think. The last thing I need right now is to do
something stupid in front of a bunch of cheerleaders.

"We were just talking about Boomer," she says as I walk up to her. "Have you heard?"

I shake my head.

"He got three days of in-school suspension," says the tall blond girl standing next to me. She throws her hair over her shoulder. "And Dr. Moody told him that if he ever pulls another stunt like stripping in school, he'll have to sit out the next two home games." The girls shake their heads, and I'm not sure if it's because they can't imagine getting three days of in-school suspension, or if they're wondering how the Gatehouse Vikings could possibly play two home football games without their best defensive tackle.

Stella narrows her eyes at me. "Rumor has it that Boomer is blaming you for what happened to him."

The blond girl twirls a piece of her hair. "Pretty brave, messing with a guy like Boomer," she says, looking me up and down. "Not bad for a sixth grader." The two girls next to her giggle and nod.

I look at Stella. "Me? Why would he blame me?"

Stella grabs the front of my T-shirt and pulls me to the side. "Listen, Charlie," she hisses into my ear, "I'm not a big fan of Boomer's, either. But if you think that trying to get revenge is the best way to be more popular around here—"

"Revenge?" I squeak. "Who said anything about revenge?"

She raises an eyebrow at me. "He pantsed you on the first

day of school. He stuffed one of your best friends into a locker. And I don't know what happened between him and Franki at the dance, but people are saying it wasn't pretty." She looks around and lowers her voice. "I don't know how you got him to strip naked, but you took it too far. Boomer's not a rocket scientist, but he's going to put two and two together and realize you had plenty of reason to get him back for the stuff he's been doing to you and your friends."

I think I'm going to puke. If Boomer Bodbreath thinks I am the reason he's sitting in suspension, I'm toast.

"Stella!" The tall blonde calls from the lunch line. "We've got your salad!"

Stella waves, then looks down at me. "Listen, Charlie. Being more popular is the best way to survive middle school. But taking on the school's biggest bully is not a good idea." She pokes the front of my shirt. "You better lie low for a while, okay?"

I'm about to tell her that lying low is what I've been trying to do all along, but she's already walking back toward the lunch line. "I want fat-free ranch!" she calls out.

■ ■ ■

For the rest of the week, my appetite stays gone, and I can't stomach more than a couple of bites of my dad's whole wheat pancakes. He makes me drink lemon balm tea instead.

Something's off with Franki, too. She stops meeting me before school and spends our lunch periods in the library, claiming she's behind on homework. On Saturday, when I stop by to see if she wants to go to the beach, no one answers the door. I decide to wander down to the soccer field instead.

When I get there, I see Grant. He's kicking ball after ball at the net, but he's missing it every time.

After a while, he looks up. "Watch this," he says when he sees me. He places the ball in the grass, backs up a foot, then runs toward it and kicks. I know he's aiming for the top right corner of the net. Instead, the ball sails over it.

"I don't get it," he mutters as much to himself as to me. "It's like I've lost my mojo."

I wonder if this has anything to do with the locker incident. Grant's ability to score is the best thing our team has going for it. Without it, the Gloucester Hurricanes are going to pummel us on Thursday.

I raise my fist in the air. "Come on, Grant!" I holler. "The next game's in five days. We need you!"

"Thanks for the reminder, pal." He jogs away from me toward the sidelines and his ball.

■ ■ ■

On Monday, I wake up to a strange noise. It doesn't take long to realize it's coming from Lucy's room. I try to sneak past it on my way downstairs, but my mom's voice stops me.

"Charlie," she says. She's sitting on the edge of my sister's bed, my dad next to her. Lucy squats on the floor in front of them. "Can you come here for a minute?"

I shuffle in.

"She's upset but won't tell us why," my dad says, his face pinchy. "Maybe you can try?"

I look at Lucy. Her brown eyes are watering, and her hair looks like it hasn't seen a brush in weeks. Every time she opens her mouth, a howl comes out. I bend down next to her.

"Lucy," I say, my voice low, "why are you acting like this?"

She stops howling and cocks her head to the side.

"It's not funny anymore," I whisper. "Can't you see you're freaking everybody out?"

She leans forward and licks my face.

"Eww!" I scream, wiping the saliva off my cheek. "You're disgusting, do you know that?"

I stand up and look at my parents. "I have no idea what's wrong with her. Good luck trying to figure it out." I march out of the room and down the stairs, grabbing a Pop-Tart from my mom's hidden stash before I bolt out the door.

■ ■ ■

Later, when I get home from school, my dad's in the kitchen, the pinched look gone.

"It took a while, but we finally figured it out," he says, smiling. "After you left, Lucy started howling again. That's when I noticed she'd lost a tooth. We looked and looked but couldn't find it anywhere." He lets out a chuckle. "Poor thing must have swallowed it in her sleep."

He steals a glance at me, but I keep my eyes on the bowl of fruit on the table. "Anyway," he continues, "I told her not to worry, that the tooth fairy would still show up. And you know what? That calmed her right down." He waves his spatula in the air like a victory salute. "See? Another Burger family crisis averted."

I just nod and grab a banana out of the bowl. My dad's grin grows.

"Wise choice, son."

"Thanks, Dad," I say. I pick up my backpack and head to my room.

CHAPTER

16

I SEE FRANKI BEFORE SHE SEES ME.

She's standing on our corner, hopping from one foot to the other. Though the air is starting to feel more like winter than fall, she isn't wearing a jacket.

I walk up behind her, not sure what to say. For more than a week, she hasn't met me here. She's even been avoiding the sixth-grade hallway.

"Hey," I say finally, tapping her on the shoulder.

She turns toward me, her lopsided grin wide and familiar. "Hey yourself." For some reason, my insides feel like I just drank hot chocolate.

"Everything okay?" I ask.

"Sure," she says, looking at me funny. "Why wouldn't it be?" She starts walking, and I do, too.

"I just . . . Well, I haven't seen you around much lately," I say. I practically have to skip to keep up with her.

"I've been busy." She sounds irritated, like this is not a topic she wants to discuss. "Did you finish the math homework?"

I nod, zipping up my jacket. "Did you?"

"Not all of it. Our power went out, and I couldn't find the flashlight."

I steal a quick look at her. The lights in my house were on all night.

She swipes a piece of hair out of her mouth with the back of her hand. "Lila didn't pay the electric bill again last month," she says matter-of-factly. "They only send three warnings."

The hot chocolate feeling turns ice-cold. "What are you going to do?" I ask.

Franki looks at me like she can't believe she's friends with such a moron. "What do you think we're going to do, Chuck? Lila will ask Mr. Richard for an advance, like always." Mr. Richard owns Wowee Hair Salon, where Franki's mom works. It's no secret that he's had a crush on her ever since she started working there. Once, he even asked her to marry him, but Franki says Lila would never marry a man who actually likes her. She married Carl instead.

"I don't guess Carl could . . . ?" I trail off, knowing before I even finish the sentence that this is the wrong thing to say.

"Could what, Chuck? Get a job? Help out? Or maybe just do something other than open beer bottles with his teeth and make fart jokes?" She throws her head back. "Do you want to know what Carl did last night when the power went off?"

I nod, not sure if I want to know or not. The prickly feeling plays at the base of my neck.

"He was sitting on the couch, finishing his fourth beer and watching *Wheel of Fortune* when the television flickered off. He was so mad that he chucked the bottle across the room and started yelling about how lousy my mother is at managing money and that she's too dim-witted to remember to pay the bills on time. Then he stormed out. Lila locked herself in her room, and I fed Rose ice cream for dinner since everything in the freezer was going to melt anyway. So no, I didn't finish the math homework."

She starts walking.

"Frank . . ." Without thinking, I reach out and grab her hand. For a second she stops and lets me hold it. We stand like that—me squeezing her fingers, and her looking like she's ready to punch something or maybe cry. Instead, she shakes herself loose from me and starts running.

"Come on, Chuck," she calls over her shoulder. "I can't afford another tardy just because you want to stand around and hold my hand all day."

■ ■ ■

On Thursday morning, Dr. Moody makes an announcement that Gatehouse is starting a chess club. I look over at Grant and grin. Pickles taught us how to play chess when we were in fourth grade, though she claims my grandfather was the master.

The notice hangs outside Mr. P's science lab: CHESS CLUB. TODAY. ALL WELCOME. My soccer game starts at six, but I only have a little bit of math homework and twenty Spanish words to memorize by tomorrow. I think about what my mom said—about expanding my horizons—and go in.

There are six people total—Grant, Dolores, and me, plus an eighth grader named Simon who keeps to himself and two seventh-grade girls whose names I still haven't learned. Mr. P stands in the front of the room, nodding as each of us walk in.

"I've already put the boards out for you, so pick a partner and sit down. You'll play for ten minutes, then move to a different table. Between matches, we'll discuss the reasons you made the moves you did, what the consequences were, and what you will do differently next time." His eyes land on me. "The beauty of chess is that it's kind of like magic. The possibilities are endless."

I plunk down opposite Grant, and we start to play. He's normally a little better than I am, but today I have him in checkmate after only six moves.

"Lucky start," I say, and we set the pieces back up. This time, I have him in checkmate after four.

"What gives?" I ask.

"What do you mean?"

"Come on, Grant," I whisper. "Something's wrong, I can tell."

His eyes shoot daggers at mine. "Oh yeah? Then why don't you clue me in, Mr. Brilliant?"

"You're playing chess like you've never seen a board before. This weekend, you were shooting like you'd never seen a soccer goal before." I glance around, but everyone's concentrating too hard to pay attention to us. "Does this have anything to do with what happened? You know"—I point toward my crotch—"Boomer and the locker?"

He stands up so fast, his kneecaps bang the board and pieces go flying. "Shut up, Burger. Just shut up. Why don't you go back to minding your own business?"

Mr. P looks up from the book he's reading but doesn't say anything.

"What's that supposed to mean?" I ask.

Grant grabs his backpack off the floor. "Exactly what it sounds like. You're usually so busy keeping a low profile, you don't have time to worry about anybody else."

"That's not true!" I say.

Mr. P looks up again. "Everything okay, gentlemen?"

Grant walks to the door. "Everything's fine. We've got our first soccer match today, and I've got to go get ready."

"But it's only three thirty," Mr. P says, looking at his watch. "Can't you stay a little longer?"

Grant shoots me a look. "Not today, Mr. P. I've got to go practice. Seems like there's a lot of people counting on me."

He storms out of the room like his pants are on fire, leaving me to pick up all the chess pieces that are now rolling onto the floor.

CHAPTER

17

WHEN I GET HOME, MY DAD'S WORKING ON HIS menu for the upcoming Cape Ann Harvest Day. Every year, his pumpkin strata and lentil stew are two of the best sellers at the festival.

As soon as I see that he's up to his elbows in pumpkin guts, my heart sinks.

"Tonight's a big game, Dad. You're coming, right?"

He wipes his hands down the front of his stiff white apron. "These stratas don't make themselves, Charlie." He smiles and taps his spoon on my nose.

I move my head away. "But it's the Gloucester Hurricanes. I was hoping you'd be there."

His face starts to pinch up. "I know, pal, but I still have a lot of work to do. I promise I'll be there next time. No matter what."

I wish I could tell him that his lentil stew tastes like dirt. Instead, I go pack my gear bag before his face can get any pinchier.

Whenever my dad is cooking, my mom is the one who gets the job of hauling us around, which means I'm almost always guaranteed to be late. Last month, I missed a dentist appointment because there was a kid with arm tattoos and a motorcycle hanging around outside the bank when we drove by. It took him twenty minutes to convince my mom that he was the bank president's nephew and was waiting to give his uncle a ride home. "You can never be too careful," she'd tried to explain as we pulled away.

Today, we make it to the field without a hitch. My mom screeches to a stop and checks her watch.

"Good luck, sweetie," she says, drumming her fingers on the steering wheel.

"What? You're not staying?"

She leans over and pats my knee. "I'm sorry, Charlie, but I can't miss this meeting with Lucy's new soccer coach. I tried to reschedule it, but he's so busy right now, you know?" I don't know, but I nod anyway. She smiles at me. "I promise I'll make it back for the second half."

I nod again and slide across the seat. I haul my bag out of the back as she throws the squad car into gear and starts to move, waving to me out the window.

I wave back, a knot growing in my stomach.

"Burger!" I hear, and look toward the field. Most of the team is already warming up, and Coach stands on the sidelines, glaring at me. I forget all about my mom and her meeting and break into a sprint.

"Well, well. If it isn't my star defender," Coach says as I plop my gear bag on the ground and bend over to double knot my cleats. I wait for him to say more, but he's already hollering at someone else.

It's no secret that Coach Crenshaw thinks soccer is a sissy sport. Four years ago, when he was hired at Gatehouse to teach eighth-grade math, he wanted to be one of the football team's coaches, but all three spots were taken. Since the soccer coach had just quit after seven seasons of finishing last in the league, Crenshaw agreed to take the team, but only until a football position opened up. He might be waiting a long time, seeing how the Gatehouse Vikings' football team has been undefeated since my parents were in middle school. My mom says someone will have to croak before one of those spots becomes available.

So that leaves a guy who hates soccer, coaching a team that stinks. Not a great combination, if you ask me.

I finish tying my cleats and start to head toward the field.

"Not so fast."

I turn and look at him, trying not to appear nervous. Coach Crenshaw can smell weakness a mile away.

He circles around, sizing me up.

"You know, Burger," he says, "I've been watching you." He stops and crosses his arms, which remind me of two greasy drumsticks. "You're a decent athlete for a scrawny kid. You got some good foot skills, and you're fast. But you know what I don't think you got?" He sneers at me. "I don't think you got any guts."

Join the club, I think, remembering what Franki had said to me.

"You paying attention, Burger?"

"Yes, sir," I say, forcing myself to look back up at him. "Heard every word."

This seems to irritate him more. "Do you think this is a joke? You think I enjoy coming out here, wasting my time, watching a kid who seems like he could not care less if he's on the field or on the bench? Well, guess what," he says, his face now uncomfortably close to mine. "I don't. Not one little bit. So, if you can't go out there and show me something new, then you might as well go home." He glares at me. "What do you say?"

I think about Dude, and how he'd handle a guy like Coach. Out of the corner of my eye, I notice the other guys have stopped their warm-up drills and now stand, watching us.

"I . . . I'll try, sir," I stammer. "I promise."

"You'll what?" He practically squeals. "You'll try?" His mouth grows so wide, I think it might split his face in two.

"Well, how about that?" He looks around in disbelief. "Did you guys hear?" He looks at my teammates, who stand like statues. "Burger here has promised to try." He starts to clap. "Maybe we should give him a medal."

A whistle blows on the field, signaling we have two minutes before the start of the game. My teammates run over and grab their gear bags, avoiding eye contact with both of us. I reach down to grab my stuff, but Coach grabs my forearm instead.

"Not so fast," he repeats, snarling. "You may be a decent athlete, Burger, but your attitude stinks. Why don't you sit this one out today."

I stare at him. Surely he's joking.

"But, Coach," I say. "We're playing the Hurricanes. I'm your best—"

It's no use. He's already walking toward the field, barking out the names of the starters and their positions. Grant glances over at me, a look of worry spreading across his face.

I pick up my gear bag. There's nothing I can do. I turn and start toward home.

■ ■ ■

It takes me less than thirty minutes to make it to my driveway, even though I walk slow. When I get there, only my dad's minivan is parked out front.

I smack my forehead, remembering. My mom is coming for the second half. She's probably pulling up to the soccer field right this minute, expecting to see me out there. What is she going to think when she realizes I'm not even there?

I'm trying to come up with a good excuse when the front door swings open and my dad walks out. His BURGER'S BEST VEGGIE BURGER apron is coated in pumpkin, and he's still carrying his spoon in one hand and the car keys in the other. He's mumbling to someone behind him.

"Come on, now," he murmurs, "it's just a short car ride. We won't be gone long, I promise."

"Dad?"

"Charlie?" He squints into the semidarkness, then smiles when he sees it's me. "You're already home."

"Uh, yeah," I stammer, glad it's too dark for him to see my face. "It was getting late, and we were really clobbering them, so the center ref called the game early." It's a crummy lie, but my dad seems to buy it. His face relaxes.

"Oh, thank goodness. Your mom called and said her meeting was running longer than she planned. I've been trying to come watch the second half, but I'm having a heck of a time getting Lucy out of the house." He looks back toward the door. Lucy squats next to it, whimpering. When she sees me, she pulls her lips back, showing me her canine teeth. I take a step backward.

"You okay?" My dad looks down at me. "You're shaking like a leaf."

"Maybe I'm coming down with something," I tell him. "I don't feel so good."

My dad puts his arm around my shoulders.

"Well, something must be going around. The way your sister's been acting tonight, I'm pretty sure she's caught something, too."

You don't know the half of it, I think as we walk back toward the house.

■ ■ ■

That night, after dinner, I take the phone to my room.

She answers on the first ring.

"Franki?"

"Yeah?"

Relief washes over me. "Your phone. It's working."

"Yeah," she says. "Aunt Carol saved the day again." Franki's aunt lives in Boston with her girlfriend and a bunch of foster dogs. She's always helping Lila out of jams.

"You don't sound too good, Chuck," Franki says. "What's up?"

It feels good to be talking to Franki again. I decide to tell her about Coach.

For a long time, she doesn't say anything. When she finally does, her voice is softer than normal.

"You know what I sometimes wish?" she says.

"What?" I press the phone closer to my ear.

"I wish that someone would invent a machine that could suck up all the jerks in this world and shoot them into outer space, far away from the rest of us." She pauses. "Charlie?"

The sound of her voice is making my eyelids heavy. "Yeah?"

"Will you do me a favor?"

I lean back on my pillow. "Okay."

"Make us a machine like that, will you? When you become a scientist?"

I close my eyes. "Sure. First thing I'll do when I get my own lab."

She giggles. "It'll probably make you famous."

"I'll get the Nobel Prize." I giggle, too. "When they give it to me, they'll say, 'To Charles Michael Burger . . . for ridding the world of worthless and unnecessarily mean, air-sucking scumbags.'"

She really cracks up at that, but then her voice gets all muffled, like she's holding her hand over the receiver. A second later, she's back, sounding like her regular Franki self.

"I've got to go."

"Now?"

"Yeah, now."

"Okay. Want to go to the beach on Saturday?"

"Can't." She sighs. "I've got to babysit Rose. Lila's doing hair and makeup for a whole wedding party. She's going to be at the shop most of the day, and I have to make sure Rose stays out of Carl's way."

"Oh," I say. "Hey, Frank?"

"Yeah?"

I pause. "Do you believe in magic?"

"Why?"

"Just curious."

She takes a deep breath. "I guess I used to. When I was a kid." I hear someone call her name. "I'll see you in the morning, okay?"

"Yeah, in the morning," I repeat, but she's already gone.

I reach over and pick my science journal off my desk.

I think about Coach and the things he said to me on the field today.

I think about Franki and her machine.

I think about magic.

I start to write.

October 1
Episode 4: The Cockroach Gets Creamed

The rumor was spreading quickly. Planet Splodii was about to be invaded by the grossest of creatures. Its ability to survive under the most impossible conditions gave it an advantage over most of the universe's inhabitants.

His name was Croach the Cockroach. But he wasn't just a cockroach. He was head of all insects throughout the galaxy, and his mission was to travel the universe looking for humans whose organs were considered a delicacy among oversize invertebrates. Once he found them, he'd stun them with his poisonous spit, then transport them back to his home, where their stomachs, livers, and intestines would be made into appetizers and their hearts and brains would be used for desserts. His poison could force a person into submission within seconds of touching someone's skin.

Dude found him chasing a group of soccer players around their practice field, his barbed tongue whipping back and forth, trying to get an accurate shot. Though the players were fast, they proved to be no match for the giant bug's six long legs, and soon he had them cornered against the field house.

"Ha-ha!" he cackled. "You will be perfect for our dinner party tonight! Now, hold still while I—"

Before he could work up a large enough loogie to coat all of them, Dude appeared. Though the bug was three times his size, Dude was smarter, faster...and more fearless.

"Okay, Croach," he said. "You've had your fun for the day. Now stop tormenting innocent people and get off my planet."

Croach's bloodshot eyes rolled back in their huge sockets.

"Who dares speak to me like that?" he screeched, turning his bulbous head sideways to get a better look.

Dude moved closer to him while the trapped players held their breaths. Dude was now directly in the bug's spitting range, a place no one in their right mind would choose to be.

"You are just an oversize bully, Croach. Without your poisonous tongue, you would be powerless. Why don't you crawl back into whatever crack you came out of before I do something you'll regret?"

The cockroach twisted his head to one side, then the other. Zeroing in on Dude, he opened his mouth, bits of drool already beginning to seep out of the sides.

"Ah, Dude Explodius." He licked his lips. "You'll make a perfect appetizer."

Dude moved quickly. As the creature's long tongue began to unroll, he shot a bolt out of the Exterminizer and into Croach's chest wall, blowing the insect into a billion particles.

Once again Planet Splodii was bug-free.

CHAPTER
18

LATER THAT NIGHT I WAKE UP, DRIPPING IN sweat. The room feels like it's August and someone cranked up the heater instead of the air conditioner.

I think back to the excuse I gave my dad. Maybe I really am coming down with something.

I sit up and scan my room. My bookshelf sags under the weight of my rock collection and favorite books, and a week's worth of T-shirts and boxers make a mountain next to my hamper. I stand up and yelp when something stabs into my foot. I turn it over. A red Lego sticks to the bottom of it.

I hop over to my desk and push aside the pile of candy wrappers that cover my journal. I open it and squint at the episode I wrote: . . . *blowing the insect into a billion particles* . . .

I shiver. Mr. P said the journal is only a catalyst. I think back to his words from the first day of school and the note that Pickles wrote me.

"Words can be powerful," I say out loud, then shake my head. Even if my science teacher knows what he's talking about, there's no way that something I write in my journal could cause my soccer coach to be blown to smithereens.

Right?

I chew on my pencil.

I'm not sure it's a chance I'm willing to take.

I erase the last part. Then I write:

> *Dude aimed for the insect. "I will spare your life, Croach, but I will render you powerless." With that, he shot a bolt of electricity straight into the bug's neck, disintegrating his poison chamber. Gasping, the cockroach coughed and sputtered, grabbing at his throat.*
>
> *"Dude," he croaked, "what have you done to me?"*
>
> *Dude glared at the pest. "I have stripped you of your one power—your poisonous tongue. Now, get off my planet before I strip you of anything else." With that, he turned toward the dining room, suddenly hungry for something salty.*

Reading back over it, I feel better. Coach Crenshaw may be a bully, but having him annihilated may be taking it a bit too far.

I walk over to my bed and climb back in, pulling the covers up over my head.

There's a lot of things I have to figure out still, but I know one thing for sure.

Dude Explodius is no murderer.

CHAPTER 19

I WAKE UP TO BARKING.

"Wroof!"

I throw the blankets off and jump up. I don't even bother to tiptoe across the squeaky floorboards. I don't care if she hears me coming.

As soon as I get to her door, I see her on all fours in the middle of her bed. Something hangs out the side of her mouth. I squint and realize it's a slobber-soaked bill with the face of Alexander Hamilton plastered across it.

Ten bucks. The tooth fairy brought my kid sister ten bucks, and she's munching on it like it's a dog biscuit.

I walk into her room.

"Lucy," I say through gritted teeth. "Give me that." She

wags her behind at me and drops the bill onto her quilt. I pick it up. One whole corner's gone.

My voice is not my own. "This isn't a joke, Lucy. I don't know if you're looking for more attention or to get me in trouble, but you need to knock it off. Now."

She jumps up and clamps her teeth down on the bill, then bolts for the bathroom.

"Lucy!" I try to grab her foot, but she's too fast. "That's real money!"

"Burgers!" My mom's voice booms up the staircase. "You've got ten minutes to be down, dressed, and ready for school. Or else!"

I don't know what *or else* means, but I prefer not to find out. I run into the hall and jump onto the banister. I practically slide right into my mom.

"Sorry," I say.

"Back it up," she says, pointing to the stairs.

"Look, Mom, I was just trying to help. Lucy was about to destroy—"

She points again, this time at my feet.

"Those are the worst toenails I've seen in a long time," she says, her face scrunched up like she just smelled the inside of my soccer bag. "I mean, really, Charlie. When's the last time you . . . Oh, never mind. Just go. Toenail clippers. March."

I jump off the banister and slump back up the stairs. Lucy

watches me as I pass by her door, and I stick my tongue out at her. She lunges, and I sprint to my room, making a mental note to myself: Always put socks on *before* breakfast.

■ ■ ■

When I get home that afternoon, my mom is sitting at the kitchen table, reading the *Cape Ann Anchor*. It comes out every Friday. She likes to read it cover to cover, starting with the police report. She makes sure every word is spelled right and no detail is missing. Then she moves on to the obituaries.

"It's important to know who's died each week," she likes to explain. "Criminals like to target the homes of bereaved families. Can you imagine?" She will shake her head like she definitely can't. "I mean, what kind of sicko would take advantage of a family during such a time?"

Today, she looks up as soon as I come in.

"You're already home?" I ask.

"I'm doing a split shift," she says. "Gargotti's got the flu, so I'm going back out tonight."

I open the fridge and peer inside.

"Charlie, come sit down for a minute."

Uh-oh. I think back to this morning. Now she probably wants to inspect my fingernails.

Instead, she pats the chair next to her and smiles. "How's school going?" she asks.

"It's fine."

"Do you like your classes?"

"They're okay."

She takes off her glasses and lays them on top of the paper. "I'm sorry, Charlie."

I blink, not expecting this. "For what?"

"For this morning," she says. "It's important that you start taking more responsibility for your personal hygiene, but I didn't have to be so hard on you."

I shrug. "They were pretty gross."

She continues as if she didn't hear me. "I know that starting middle school can be a big adjustment. Growing up can be tough and—"

"I'm fine, Mom."

She nods, but her face is still frowning. "Okay. I'm sorry— I just worry, that's all."

I fiddle with the pen in front of me. "Maybe you worry too much."

"Maybe it's part of my job description." She grins. "I think it's on the list, right below making dentist appointments and buying Christmas presents."

I laugh. "It should definitely be below buying Christmas presents."

Just then the back door flies open, and Stella storms in. Dark stains cover the front of her cheerleading uniform, and dirt-colored water drips from her hair. She looks like she's been shot with a mud gun.

"Mom!" she wails. "Look what the mail truck just did to me!"

My mom jumps up and grabs Stella's arm. "Come on. We need to soak that sweater before the stains set." She starts to steer my sister out of the room but stops in the doorway and winks at me. "And laundry. Add that to my job description list."

CHAPTER

20

I WAKE UP EARLY SATURDAY MORNING, BUT instead of heading to the basement and the TV, I head to the laundry room. Shoving a week's worth of clothes into the washing machine, I turn it on, dumping what seems like the right amount of detergent inside. Next, I grab a rag and some cleaning supplies. Twenty minutes later, my shelves are dusted, my bed is made, and every Lego has been picked up off the floor and dumped into a box, along with my rock collection and my Matchbox cars. I look around and smile.

I'm carrying the box downstairs when Stella comes out of the kitchen. She stops and leans against the wall.

"What's that?" she asks, eyeing the box.

"Just stuff," I say.

"What kind of stuff?"

"Stuff that I don't need anymore," I say. "Kid stuff."

"Put it in the basement storage room," she says, walking to the hall closet. She opens the door and pulls out my mom's leather jacket, the one she knows she's not supposed to wear. "That's where Mom likes to keep those things."

"Since when?"

"Since forever, I guess. A couple of weeks ago, I found her down there rifling through a box of our old baby clothes." She turns sideways, studying herself in the hall mirror. "At first, I thought she looked upset, but when she saw me, she said she was just trying to figure out what was worth keeping and what she should send to the holiday clothing and toy drive at the precinct this year."

"Oh," I say. I can't imagine my mom being upset over a bunch of baby clothes.

Suddenly, Stella's face lights up. "It's inventory morning at Pickles's store, remember? You coming?" She tugs on my sweatshirt, her voice cheery. "It'll be so fun."

I look at my sister, knowing exactly what she's up to. Stella figures by getting me to come along, she'll have someone she can boss around all day. My sister wants those cheerleading shoes, but she doesn't want to actually work for them.

"Nah," I say, opening the door to the basement. "I've got other things to do."

"What kind of things?" she says, the cheer gone.

"Important things," I say.

"Suit yourself," she says, "she'll be here in five minutes if you change your mind."

At the bottom of the stairs, I open the door to the storage room. In front of me are stacks of boxes, each with something written on the outside in black marker. I shove over a box labeled DRESS-UP CLOTHES and slide mine in next to it. I'm about to close the door when I think of something. I grab a marker off the shelf and scribble: CHARLIE'S STUFF—NOT FOR TOY DRIVE! on the outside.

I may be too old for Legos and my rock collection, but that doesn't mean I want some other kid to have them.

I hear panting and turn around. Lucy's sitting in my favorite spot, watching *Scooby-Doo* cartoons. Her head is cocked to one side as she follows the images across the screen. She's chewing on my soccer cleat.

I walk over, ready to rip the shoe out of her mouth, when Stella yells from upstairs.

"Charlie! Pickles is here! Last chance!"

I look at Lucy. She lets out a low growl.

"Wait up!" I say, leaning over. It takes some tugging, but eventually I pry the shoe from her jaws. She starts howling as I make for the stairs, taking them two at a time.

With Franki babysitting all day and Lucy playing king of the couch, spending the morning at Pickles's store doesn't sound so bad. Even if I am going to get bossed around.

Stella doesn't boss me around. For three hours, she does nothing but eat cinnamon jelly beans and text her friends. When Pickles comes out of her office, my sister stuffs her head inside a box and mutters something about how we need to find a place to put the board games and jigsaw puzzles.

"You all have done some fine work," Pickles says, looking around. "I never could have done this alone."

Even without Stella's help, I've managed to get most of the boxes unpacked, sorted, and organized in the stock room. My stomach growls, and I realize it must be close to lunchtime.

As if she can read my thoughts, Pickles winks at me.

"Ready for the deli?"

Stella blows a piece of hair out of her face. "Sounds fantastic—I'll meet you guys out back." She grabs her purse, then heads off toward the bathroom.

Pickles rolls her eyes, then smiles at me. "Can you grab my wallet from the office? I'll just lock the front door, and we'll be on our way." I nod and follow my sister toward the back of the store.

In the office, I spot her wallet on the desk. I'm just about to grab it, when I notice a photograph lying next to it. I pick it up.

"It's your grandfather."

I jump. Pickles stands in the doorway. "I was going through

some old papers and found it." She nods at me. "Thought you might like to have it."

I study it closely. His hair is thick, but white as snow, and his eyes are the same green as mine. He grins at me like he's got some great secret he's dying to share.

Pickles walks over to me. "This was taken in his lab at Harvard. He loved that lab—would sleep there if I'd let him." I look at the picture again. He's leaning against a table, a row of beakers lined up behind him. His arm rests on something, a pad of paper, maybe, or a notebook—

"Pickles, did Gramps have a journal?"

"Yes, he did," she says. "He loved that thing, almost like it was a part of him. Took it everywhere he went."

My pulse quickens. If I can get my hands on Gramps's journal, maybe it will help answer some questions about mine. "Do you still have it?" I ask her. "The journal?"

She shakes her head.

"Unfortunately, no. During the accident there was a fire. Almost everything in his lab was destroyed, including the journal."

"Did you ever read it?"

She smiles, but her face seems sad. "No, but sometimes I wish I had. He was so attached to it that I always wondered if there was more on those pages than just science data. It was as if his very existence was somehow tied to what was inside that journal."

I flop down onto the chair, something inside me deflating. What if Gramps's journal had been a catalyst, too? Mr. P said that maybe this gift runs in—

I sit up, thinking of something else. "Pickles," I say, grabbing her arm. "Did Gramps ever tell you who gave him the journal?"

She nods. "A teacher." She looks down at the photo. "Your grandfather said he was the person who taught him what it meant to be a true scientist."

My heart flutters in my chest. "Do you know what happened to him? To the teacher, I mean."

She chuckles. "That was a long time ago, Charlie. I'm sure he's long gone by now."

My stomach rumbles, but I reach in my back pocket and pull the now-crumpled piece of paper out.

"'Words can be powerful,'" I read. "'Believe in their magic and anything can happen.'" I look up. "You left this on my computer. Why?"

She closes her eyes. "It was something your grandfather used to say whenever he was wrestling through a difficult experiment or working on a new invention. He said someone special had shared it with him when he was young. I thought I'd share it with you."

Just then, Stella appears in the doorway.

"Hey, guys! Everyone ready to—Oh!" She stops and points a long fingernail at me. "What's wrong with him?"

Pickles waves her off. "Just hungry, that's all." Stella walks over and puts a hand on my forehead, and I don't have the energy to swat it away.

"You look like death," she says. "Maybe we should call—"

"He's fine," Pickles says, pulling me out of the chair. She throws an arm over each of our shoulders. "After a few ham on rye sandwiches, we'll all feel as good as new!"

CHAPTER

21

VIKINGS ARE NUMBER ONE!

It's Monday afternoon, and the banner hanging from the side of the bus announces our fake confidence as we roll down Route 128 to our biggest game of the season. The Peabody Patriots have been the district champs for three years in a row. With an offense that can score from midfield and a goalie named Mark "Hands Man" Mansfield, they are unstoppable.

That is, I hope, until today.

"Grant?" I poke the lump sitting next to me. Grant can't make it for more than five minutes in a moving vehicle before he's sound asleep, his head lolling against the window and his mouth wide open. It normally makes him a crummy seat partner, but today it's exactly what I need.

I reach into my gear bag and pull out my journal.

I've got work to do.

I showed up at school early again this morning, hoping to catch Mr. P before the first bell. I had more questions, ones that had been rolling around in my head since Saturday.

Was he the science teacher who had given my grandfather his journal?

Was it a catalyst like mine?

But when I got to Mr. P's room, the door was locked. I peeked in. Beakers lined the back counter, and stools were scooted neatly under the lab tables. Nothing looked out of the ordinary.

I went to the front office. Ms. Carson, the secretary, shook her head as soon as I said his name.

"Terrible tragedy for Mr. Perdzock. There was a death in his family over the weekend. He's off to retrieve the body."

"Retrieve the body?" My throat tightened. "Where?"

"Not sure. He said something about an island in the Pacific." She peered at me over the top of her glasses. "Look, kid, when someone calls in sick, my job is to track down a substitute, not keep track of the teacher."

I thought about what Stella said, about how Mr. P would leave for somewhere exotic around fall break. I started to sweat. He couldn't leave now. Not when I finally had some questions to ask.

"All right, boys!" Coach's voice booms at us from the front of the bus. "You got ten minutes until show time!"

I flip open my journal, knowing I have to hurry.

After my visit with Ms. Carson this morning, I headed straight to the eighth-grade hallway. I realized that if Mr. P wasn't around to answer my questions about Gramps, I needed to try to get some answers about Coach. If I hadn't changed that last journal entry in time, Ms. Carson might be looking for a substitute for him, too.

As I rounded the corner, Linda Prattsworth, a cheerleader, was coming out of the math room.

Mere mortals don't talk to Linda. Especially not sixth-grade ones like me.

"Um . . . hi . . . Linda, it's Charlie Burger." I shot her a smile that I hoped was more charming than cheesy. "Stella's brother?"

Her movie-star lips turned downward. "Stella has a brother?"

"Never mind that," I said. "I saw you coming out of Mr. Crenshaw's room just now. Did you notice anything strange about him today?" I paused. "Like, was he acting funny, or did he sound different?"

She cocked her head to one side. "Why are you talking to me?"

That did it. I beat it out of there faster than she could recite her locker combination.

Now, hearing Coach's voice, it's obvious that nothing's changed. Coach is fine. His voice is, too.

I have to try something else. If I don't, we're sure to get pummeled by the Patriots. Not only did we lose the game he made me sit out, but according to Grant, Coach screamed so much that one guy started crying and another puked right in the middle of the field. And as for Grant? I heard his shots didn't even come close to the net.

Grant needs this win. We all need this win.

I take a deep breath and start writing. I've made a decision. I hope it's the right one.

October 5

Episode 5: An Intergalactic Space Scum Scramble

He was halfway through his double chocolate pudding cake and his third comic book when he heard trouble from the field below. He frowned. Was Croach back? Even though he hadn't exterminated the cockroach, Dude was sure he had taught him a lesson. Would he dare step foot on Planet Splodii again?

But it wasn't Croach. It was the voice of Grangor, Dude's closest ally and friend.

Grabbing his cape, he took off, knowing he only had seconds to spare. Grangor was smart and fast, but since he was human, he was less than half the size of any intergalactic space scum. Something was threatening Planet Splodii again, and this time it was Grangor who was in trouble.

Thanks to Dude's supersonic speed, he made it in record time.

As he rounded the corner, he saw them. Five space cadets from a rival planet had cornered Grangor, pushing him up against the wall, blocking his path and preventing him from running. Though he kept calling for help, no one was a match for these guys.

Except, of course, Dude Explodius.

"Okay, scum. Party's over," Dude announced, tossing them aside like rag dolls. One by one, they hit the hard ground, then crawled backward, out of his path.

His comrade looked up.

"Dude Explodius." He sighed. "Once again, you came through for me. I was about to be lunch for a bunch of galactic—"

"You can thank me later," Dude growled. "Right now, you've got work to do! Now go and

"Okay, everyone, off the bus!" Coach barks. "This ain't a trip to the nail salon."

I cringe when I see how little I've written. I doubt it's enough, but I'm out of time.

"Let's go, let's go," he says, motioning for us to file toward the front. "And don't look so terrified. It's just soccer."

I reach for my gear bag just as Grant opens his eyes. He spies my journal.

"What're you carrying that around for?" he asks, nodding at it.

I shrug and stuff it into my bag. "No reason. Come on, man. You don't want to be the dweeb who has to run laps in front of the whole field, do you?"

He gets up to follow me, but not before peeking out the window. The Patriots file off the bus next to us. "Oh, man," he mutters, watching them. "Those guys are huge. We are in. For. It."

Not if I can help it, I think.

CHAPTER

22

THIRTY SECONDS LEFT IN THE FIRST HALF, and we've held the Patriots at 0–0. Grant's had four shots on goal—and he's aimed each one right at Hands Man. The six-foot goalie hasn't even broken a sweat.

I, on the other hand, am swimming in the stuff. Every time I stop to catch my breath, another Patriot barrels toward me, juking to the left, the right, trying to find my weakness, a hole that he can slip through. Beads of sweat hang from my hair and drip into my eyes, but I refuse to sub out.

Twice I scan the stands, but don't see my parents. I look for Franki, thinking she might have caught a ride with someone, but she's not there, either.

The ref's long whistle signals the end of the first half, and I have to practically crawl off the field, my body a piece of rubbery spaghetti. My teammates follow, grabbing for water bottles and slapping backs. Everyone's feeling pretty proud of how we've managed to hold off the Patriots so far. Until Coach steps up.

"You guys think that score means something?" he says, pacing back and forth in front of our bench. "These guys are just playing with you, waiting for the right moment to make their move. It's like a game of cat and mouse out there." He looks right at me. "You're no match for them—and if you don't see that, then you're more clueless than I thought."

We keep our heads down, our chins practically sticking to the front of our wet jerseys.

He continues to pace in front of us, his voice almost cheery. "Maybe your parents can get some of their soccer fees back once the officials realize Gatehouse signed a bunch of girls to play on the boys' team. Bet that would be a relief, huh?"

At the mention of parents, I look over at the crowd again. And that's when I see her, my mom, squeezed in between David O'Leary's dad and some other guy I don't recognize. She's on her phone, but she waves.

A smile tugs at the corners of my mouth. I knew she wouldn't miss another game.

"You think this is funny, Burger?"

Uh-oh.

"Why don't you come over here and let us all in on your little joke."

The bench shifts beneath me, and I realize someone has stood up.

"Leave him alone."

Eighteen heads snap up. Who would interrupt Coach Crenshaw when he's on a roll?

Grant stands in front of our bench, his fists balled at his sides.

A small groan creeps out from some place deep inside me, and I feel my gut take a nose dive. I glance back up at the stands. My mom is off the phone and pointing me out to the guy next to her. I look at Grant again.

"Grant," I hiss, "don't do this. Not now."

It's no use. He's just getting started.

"I'm sick of your insults, Coach," he says, his voice almost steady. "We need you to coach us, not holler at us all the time. Just because we're not football players, doesn't mean we don't count. We're not going to take it anymore."

The guy next to me makes a sound like he's being squeezed too tight. Someone farther down the bench starts whimpering.

Coach bends down, his back to the crowd. His eyes shoot bullets into Grant's.

"Why don't you start over?" Coach growls. "But this time, say it nice and slow so I don't miss a single word."

"I . . . I . . ." Grant sputters. "I just wanted to—"

Coach reaches out and grabs his jersey, twisting it in his fist. I glance around. No one seems to notice except my teammates, who sit wide-eyed, the blood draining from their faces.

Coach's next words run through my veins like ice water.

"You just wanted to *what?*" Coach sputters, spit flying everywhere. "Don't talk to me about wants, Gupta."

I close my eyes. My skin crackles and pops.

"You want to know what I want?"

I hear someone snicker beside me.

And then a giggle.

"For starters, I never wanted to—"

Coach's voice is rising like he's been sucking on a helium balloon. First one octave, then another. I open my eyes and look around. It's happening! My journal entry about Coach worked! Everyone else hears it, too.

It takes a minute before he notices. He stops—midsentence—clears his throat, then tries again. He lets go of Grant, who flops to the ground like a rag doll. Clawing at his neck, Coach coughs and sputters, but it's no use. His voice is nothing more than a squeak.

The referee blows the whistle, waving at us to get back onto the field. Dexter Honeycutt, our team captain, is doubled over with laughter next to me. He's supposed to be calling out our field positions, but he's laughing so hard, I'm afraid he's going to pass out.

The ref is losing patience. "Vikings!" he calls out. "I need your starting line! Halftime's over!"

A couple of us turn to Coach, but he's useless, too. He's bouncing around like a pogo stick, cursing and squeaking and shaking his head.

A sharp whistle. The Patriots glare at us from the field. "Vikings!"

I turn to my team. "Okay, same formation as before," I bark, pointing at the guys like I do this all the time. "Dave, you're center-mid. Josh and Jared, you guys take the wings. Grant?" I look around to see if he's okay, but he's already sprinting across the field.

"I've got it covered, Burger!" He shoots me a thumbs-up over his shoulder. "You just worry about protecting our goal, and we'll be fine!" He gets to the midline and squares his shoulders, staring into the face of the Patriots' top striker.

In the end, we're better than fine. We're unbelievable.

Thirty-five minutes later the final whistle blows.

The score? Three to zero, Vikings.

Grant scored every goal.

Hands Man Mansfield never had a chance.

CHAPTER

23

TUESDAY NIGHT TURNS OUT TO BE PIZZA
night at our house. And I'm not talking the whole-wheat-
pizza-with-soy-cheese-and-tofu-pepperoni kind of pizza that
my dad likes to make. Tonight it's the real deal.

Any time my dad has a catering gig, I invite Franki over,
and we order in from House of Pizza. My mom says our kitchen
can only handle one cook, and she's not interested in compet-
ing for the job.

Franki and I are sitting on the porch, waiting for the deliv-
ery guy to show up. As soon as we hear him rattling up the
hill in his beat-up Toyota, we fly down the steps and grab
the boxes before he can get out of the car.

"Pizza's here!" I holler as we run into the kitchen. Stella

stands by the counter, her phone in one hand and a Diet Coke in the other.

"Stop screaming," she says, not looking up. "Mom's napping, remember?"

"Why's she napping?" Franki asks, grabbing two cans of root beer out of the fridge while I flip open a pizza box. "Your mom never naps."

"She's been in bed since we got home today," Stella whispers as my mom rounds the corner. I'm licking a piece of cheese off my hand, but I stop when I see her face.

"Jeez, Mom. You don't look so good."

She grabs a coffee cup, then rummages around in the fridge until she pulls a bottle of wine out of the back. "I'm fine. Just feeling a little run-down."

Stella and I exchange a look. Run-down? More like run-over. Her hair is matted on one side, and she's in her bathrobe even though it's only six thirty. Plus, she's drinking alcohol, which she never does, except on special occasions. That bottle has probably been stuck back there since New Year's Eve.

She uncorks it and fills the coffee cup to the brim.

Stella looks up from her phone. "You okay?"

Mom looks from Stella to Franki to me. She takes a long drink from her mug. "I will be."

Her cell phone rings, and she jumps up, taking it and the mug with her.

"What's gotten into her?" Stella asks.

"How should I know?" I say, wiping my mouth with the back of my shirtsleeve. "She seemed fine after the game yesterday." I grab another piece of pizza.

After a minute or two, my mom walks back in the room, her cell phone stuck to her ear.

"I appreciate your time, Chief, and I can assure you, this will never happen again." She takes a long drink from the mug, then nods. "Yes, sir . . . yes, I understand. Okay, good night."

She sets down her phone, staring at it like she's never seen it before.

"Mom?"

"It was a simple misunderstanding," she says. "I was just trying to do the right thing."

Stella rolls her eyes at me, then goes back to texting. We've heard these words before.

"What happened, Mrs. Burger?" Franki asks.

My mom sighs. "I was on my way to the early bird boxing class at the gym this morning and decided to take a shortcut through the Ellison Estates. I was driving by those houses— you know, the ones everyone calls the McMansions?—when something caught my eye."

Franki scoots to the edge of her seat, while Stella's eyes stay glued to her phone. I reach for my third slice.

"What did you see?" Franki asks.

"A figure dressed all in black was climbing through a small window on the side of the Huffingtons' place. I pulled my squad car around to the back and cut the engine, watching while the suspect slipped inside."

"Wow." Franki whistles. "You must have been terrified."

"An officer of the law learns to combat her fears," my mom says, tilting the mug to her mouth.

Franki's mouth hangs open. "So, what happened next?"

"I radioed for an on-duty officer and waited. After a few minutes, though, I couldn't just sit there. What if the Huffingtons were home, slumbering away, while some madman was loose in their home? I grabbed my gun belt off the seat and snapped it on, then crept up onto the deck. I was peeking through the back window when I saw him, a dark figure moving through the kitchen."

Franki's eyes are so big, I'm pretty sure they're going to fall out and roll onto my slice of pizza. "And then what?"

"I rapped on the window with the butt of my gun," she says. "You know, just to get his attention. But as soon as the suspect saw me, he took off toward the front stairs. I couldn't just stand there, now could I?"

Franki shakes her head. I grab her root beer and take a long swig.

"So, did you catch him?"

"Not exactly. Turns out the suspect was the Huffingtons' oldest daughter, Mary Elizabeth. She had gone out early to get the paper. When she got back, she realized she had forgotten her house key, so she decided to climb through the window instead of waking her parents. Not very smart, if you ask me."

Actually, Mary Elizabeth Huffington is very smart. She graduated from Columbia last year, but I don't remind my mom of that. I finish Franki's root beer instead.

"But why did she run?" Franki scratches her head like she's a detective on one of those cop shows. "You're a police officer."

My mom runs her index finger around the inside of her coffee mug, then licks it off. "She claims that my orange track-suit confused her. She thought *I* was the intruder and had escaped from prison. Can you imagine?"

Franki shakes her head like she definitely can't. I'm just about to ask what's for dessert when Lucy appears in the doorway.

"Ruff!" she says, wagging her backside.

Great, I think. *Now what?*

She jumps up onto her chair and tries to lick my mother's hand.

"Lucy!" my mom scolds. "That's gross."

I decide to start a new subject. "How about that game yesterday, huh, Mom? Could you believe that second half? You know, we have another one this week."

My mom picks at a chip on her mug. "I'll try to make it, Charlie, but I can't promise anything." She lowers her voice.

"I'm working two night shifts, and I have an appointment for Lucy with Dr. Daniels this week."

We all look at my kid sister, who's trying to eat her pizza without using her hands.

"Who's Dr. Daniels?" asks Stella, not looking up.

"A child psychologist."

I choke on a piece of cheese.

"Like, a shrink?"

"No, not a shrink." My mom glares at me. "He is an expert in anxiety and behavioral issues, especially with young girls who have had some family dynamic challenges."

"Huh?"

My mom lowers her voice some more. "Your father and I think this . . . behavior of Lucy's . . . may be your sister's way of dealing with stress."

I blink. "You think Lucy's under stress?"

"Yes, we do." She sits back and crosses her arms. "And we think there are things we as a family can do to help alleviate it for her."

I can't believe this. "Mom, she's ten. What kind of stress could she possibly be under?"

Franki points her pizza crust at me, her mouth full. "Ten can be tough, Charlie."

I roll my eyes as my mom beams at Franki. As if on cue, Lucy lets out a whine.

"What is it, honey?" my mom asks her.

We all watch while she tries to pick up her pizza with her teeth. She misses, and it falls into her lap.

"Oops," Franki says.

My mom drops her head into her hands. I decide this is not the right time to ask if she bought Twinkies for dessert.

Later, when Franki and I are playing Zombie Smasher, she presses pause on her controller and turns to me, her eyes dead serious.

"Lucy does seem to be acting pretty strange lately," she says. "What do you think is going on with her?"

I try to shoot a fireball at the zombies coming toward me, but it's no use. Without Franki's help, they surround me, and I'm toast within twenty seconds. I throw my controller onto the coffee table and look at her, irritated.

"How should I know?" I snap. "Maybe my whole family is just strange."

Franki throws her head back, laughing.

"What's so funny?" I ask her.

"Chuck," she says, slapping my thigh, "your family at its strangest is more normal than my family any day!"

CHAPTER 24

OVER **THE NEXT** FOUR **WEEKS,** THINGS START to feel pretty normal again. Sure, Lucy's still pretending she's a dog, but Coach has gone back to ignoring me most of the time, and Franki's acting more like her old self. I start to relax, thinking maybe sixth grade isn't going to be so bad after all.

But then it happens. It's the Wednesday before fall break, a morning that's cold enough to make my nose hairs stick together every time I sniff. I get that uh-oh feeling as soon as I see Franki. She's already waiting at our spot, and her face is scrunched up in a frown.

"You okay?" I ask. I blow on my fingers, which are already numb.

She keeps her eyes glued to her sneakers. "Lila wants to send me to Colorado for fall break."

I laugh. "And my mom wants to send me to Mars."

Her frown grows.

"Hey," I say, grabbing her arm. "I was just joking."

"I wasn't."

I stop grinning. "Why Colorado?"

"My dad is there."

This is one of the things I can't stand about Franki Saylor. For a girl who usually can't shut up, she has a way of leaving out the important stuff. Like the fact that she has a dad.

"You told me your dad was dead."

"I did?"

I jump in front of her.

"We were nine," I say. "At the Sweet Spot. You told me your dad died in a plane crash. We were eating Dinosaur Crunch ice cream. You had on orange high-tops and a yellow T-shirt."

"So I lied. Sue me."

"Franki . . ." I grip her arm, like maybe I can squeeze the truth out.

"He didn't die, okay?" she whispers. "He left. Nobody told me why, and I never asked. He lives in Colorado now, with a new wife and new kids and a dog."

I let go of her, and we start walking.

For a minute, neither of us says anything.

"So, why now?" I finally ask.

"I don't know. Lila said . . ." Her voice trails off.

I wait, but she doesn't go on.

"Do you want to?" I ask. "Go, I mean?"

"No. Yes. Maybe. I don't know." She shakes her head. "I don't even remember what he looks like, Chuck. And Colorado is so far away from Rose." She stares down at her feet. "But maybe it'll beat hanging around here."

For some reason, this stings. I kick a rock out of my way.

We walk in silence for a few minutes. When we get to the corner, she stops and turns to me.

"I'm scared, Charlie."

I give her arm a playful punch. "Come on, Franki. You're the bravest person I know. You're not scared of anything."

Her voice gets smaller. "What if they don't like me?"

"They will."

"How do you know?"

"Because you're you," I say. "You're the coolest person I know."

A tiny smile plays on her lips. "You're just saying that because you're my best friend."

"I'm just saying it because it's true."

And then, without warning, she leans in and puts her lips on my earlobe. She smells like syrup.

"Thanks, Charlie."

We start walking again, and I have to remind myself to breathe. When we get to the courtyard, the wind is whipping leaves around everyone's ankles, and the bare maple trees rock back and forth. I look up at the sky—dark angry clouds roll in off the ocean. A storm is approaching.

The words fall out of me before I can stop them. "Or maybe you could stay. We'll have a bonfire on the beach. My dad will take us out to Lobster Cove, and we can look for—"

"It's only for a week, Charlie."

"I know." I shove my hands in my pockets. "It's just that . . ."

"What?"

I can't look at her. "What if you like it so much, you don't want to come back?"

She laughs. "I don't think I have a choice," she says, then slugs the top of my arm. "Plus, I have to come back. You wouldn't know what to do without me."

And with that, she takes off running.

"Franki!" I call after her, but she's gone, and I can't do anything to stop her.

Or can I?

November 4

Episode 6: Dude to the Rescue

The female earthling stood in his doorway, staring at the starcraft in front of her. It was there to take her back to her people, people she had run away from when she escaped to Planet Splodii.

"Stay here," he commanded, his voice deep and full of awesomeness.

"I can't," she whispered, her eyes all gooey like a hot fudge sundae. "They're making me go back."

"I will make it so that you don't have to," Dude promised.

"Oh, Dude Explodius," she sighed. "Can you? I would like nothing better than to just stay here with you. You are my hero."

He grunted, then turned his attention to the starcraft.

Dude closed his eyes, aiming the Exterminizer at the craft's engine panel. After a jolt and a small explosion, he opened his eyes. The craft was grounded, and it would take years before the earthling's people would be able to send another one. She was safe for now.

CHAPTER

25

THURSDAY MORNING, FRANKI IS ALL SMILES.

"The decision's been made," she says, blowing on her hands. "I'm definitely going."

I think about the journal entry I wrote last night and feel a little queasy.

"Are you sure?"

She nods. "My dad is sending the itinerary today. I'm flying as an unaccompanied minor." She says the last two words with such importance you'd think she'd just said *Secret Service*. "Do you know what an unaccompanied minor is, Chuck?"

"No clue."

She sends me a sideways glance. "It's when you're not old enough to fly by yourself so a flight attendant is in charge of you the whole time. It's like having your own personal assistant."

I let out a snort. "When are you leaving?"

"Friday."

"*Friday?*" I stop. "As in tomorrow?"

She looks away. "I guess my dad and Lila have been planning this for a while, but they wanted to keep it a secret until right before it was time to go. I was kind of sore at Lila when she told me, but now I understand why." Her voice gets lower. "Carl got mad when he found out I was going. He said my father likes to throw his money around, and he should've been throwing it toward more child support, not fancy plane tickets." She picks at a hole in her coat. "When I pointed out that the last child support check got spent on new tires for his truck, he about came unglued." She looks up at me. "It's probably best for everyone if I get out of here for a little while."

A sharp pain starts to grow in my belly. Maybe I shouldn't have written that entry after all.

"I talked to my dad on the phone last night, Chuck," she says. "He told me all about his boys and how excited they are to meet me and that his wife bought new sheets for the guest room." She grins. "A room just for guests . . . Can you imagine?"

I shake my head, like I really can't.

"And you know what else? My dad said we're going to the mountains for a few days, and they're going to teach me how to ski. Me! Skiing!"

I try to smile, but the pain in my gut is getting worse.

"Hey," she says, looking over at me, "are you going to throw up?"

"I'm fine," I say.

"Okay. Because all of a sudden, you look kind of pale."

"I'm fine," I say again. "What time are you leaving?"

"After school tomorrow. Lila's taking the train into Boston with me." She stuffs her hands into her pockets. "I'm kind of nervous."

"About flying?"

She shakes her head. "About seeing him again. It's been so long, and I have so many questions."

"About why he left?"

"About why he didn't come back." She kicks at a chunk of ice. "Leaving is one thing. It's the staying gone I don't get."

The pain jabs my side.

"Chuck? You sure you're okay?"

I nod and walk faster. I've got to get rid of that last entry.

■ ■ ■

When I get to school, I head straight to my locker and plunk down onto the floor next to it. Grabbing my journal out of my backpack, I'm ready to erase the last entry, but I stop. I think about the last time I erased something, and how it didn't work right away. I mean, sure, Coach Crenshaw eventually lost his voice, but it took longer than I expected. What if erasing my words doesn't work in time? Franki's plane leaves tomorrow. She has to be on it. She has to make it to Colorado.

Since I can't talk to Mr. P, there's only one other person who might be able to help me fix things for Franki. But first, I'll need some help from my sister.

I spot Stella right away. Her back is pressed up against her locker while some beefy guy I don't recognize leans against her. Her eyes are closed, and his face is just inches from hers.

"Stella," I hiss.

"Charlie?" She opens one eye. "What're you doing here?"

"Uh . . ." I say, trying not to stare at the bulging biceps in front of me. "I need to talk to you."

Beefy Guy turns around, my sister's lip gloss all over his face. "Who're you?"

This is worse than facing Linda the cheerleader.

I talk quickly, trying not to look either of them in the eyes.

"I need to borrow your cell phone. I'll bring it back after first period."

Her tone turns icy. "What for?"

"I need to call Dad," I say, thinking fast. "I left my math homework at home."

"We only got five minutes before first bell rings," Beefy whines, clearly annoyed that his face-sucking time is being wasted on me.

Stella reaches in her back pocket and pulls out her phone.

"You really need to work on being more responsible, Charlie. Forgetting your homework is not—"

"I got it, thanks," I say, grabbing the phone from her hand. I sprint down the hall to the boys' bathroom, knowing I don't have much time.

■ ■ ■

I pull the stall door closed and look under the partition to make sure no one else is in the bathroom. When I know the coast is clear, I scan the contacts until I find Pickles.

Come on, Pickles, I think. *Answer. Please answer.*

She does on the third ring.

"Stella?" Her voice is still raspy, like she hasn't talked to anyone since she woke up. "That you, baby?"

"Pickles, it's Charlie." My words come out fast, tumbling over one another. "I only have a few minutes, but I have a question. An important one."

She seems to get it. Instead of asking me to slow down or why I'm calling on a school morning, she just sighs. "I'll give it a shot," she says.

But now that I have her on the phone, I don't know where to start. I want to ask more about Gramps and his journal, but I've got to try to fix things for Franki first. "Pickles . . ." I say, closing my eyes. "Remember when you told me that you always thought maybe Gramps was writing stuff in his journal that was more than just science data?"

"Uh-huh," she says sleepily.

"Well, did you ever see him *erase* something he wrote in it?"

She's silent for a minute. "I don't know, Charlie. . . . Gramps was pretty secretive about everything he wrote in there. I do remember one time, though—"

The bell rings.

"One time what?" I press.

"I saw him rip a page out and throw it in the trash can." She chuckles. "I thought about trying to sneak a peek, but you know what that crazy coot did?"

I grip the phone tighter. "What?"

"He lit a match and threw it on top of that page—set the whole can on fire." Her voice trails off. "Could've burned the whole place down, but instead he just set off the smoke alarm."

"Pickles, I've got to go now."

"Is everything okay?" she asks.

"I don't know. But I think I'm about to find out."

We hang up, and I pull the journal out of my bag. I flip to the entry about Franki and grab the top of the page, ripping it out of the notebook. I crumple it up and lob it toward the trash can. It misses.

I walk over and pick it up. Even though I want to make sure Franki gets to Colorado, I'm not willing to light the trash can on fire. Instead, I toss the paper into the can and hurry off to class.

After school I show up to chess club to find a note taped to Mr. P's door:

To the Gatehouse Middle School Chess Club,
Mr. Perdzock will not be here for today's meeting. He would like me to remind you that you have a tournament coming up soon and to always drink upstream from the herd. Regards, Ms. Carson.

We shuffle inside and stake out our seats.

Grant pulls a cloth board from his bag. I watch while he places the white pieces on his side then hands me the black ones.

Seven moves later we are still even. Ever since our win against the Patriots, Grant's confidence has quadrupled. He captures my queen on his next move.

"Hey, Burger?"

"Yeah?" I study the board, knowing that if I'm not careful, he'll have me in checkmate soon.

"Have you noticed anything—I don't know—*different* about yourself lately?"

My stomach does a little sideways flip. I move my bishop. "No. Have you?"

"Yeah." He takes my bishop with his knight. "Something big."

I swallow hard. "And?" I say, lowering my voice.

"And," he says, "I don't get why you haven't talked to me about it." He looks over his shoulder. "It's pretty awesome, actually."

I take a deep breath and move my other bishop.

"I don't know what—"

"Listen, Burger." His eyes grow bigger. "I get it."

"You do?"

He smiles, his teeth bright white against his dark skin. "Well, sure. And, it's not like you're the first guy to ever be in this predicament."

"I'm not?"

"Of course not." He shakes his head and captures my knight with his rook. "Lots of guys have been where you are. Me, for one."

My hand freezes. I hadn't thought about this. Maybe I'm not the only kid at Gatehouse whose journal is some sort of catalyst. Mr. P never mentioned it, but that doesn't mean there aren't others having the same weird experiences, right?

Grant continues. "It started a few weeks ago." He glances over at Dolores, who's digging at something lodged in her front teeth. "Though, unlike Franki, I'm not sure the feelings are mutual."

I look up at him. "What's Franki got to do with this?"

He reaches across the table and slaps my arm. "Don't worry, Burger, your secret's safe with me. And, in all honesty, I think Franki's got it bad for you, too." He looks at Dolores again and sighs. "You're lucky. Mine is a love that is still unrequited."

I slam my chess piece down on the board and dig my fingers into my scalp. "Jeez, Grant. I thought you were talking about . . . Oh, never mind." I can't decide if I should be relieved that Grant doesn't know about the journal or mad that he's talking about Franki and me like that. "Franki's my best friend. What you're suggesting is just plain wrong."

A smile creeps across Grant's face. He's clearly getting a kick out of this.

"Deny it all you want, Charlie Burger, but the truth is written all over your lovesick mug." He shakes his head like he's worried for me. "You're a mess, my friend."

I'm about to make a mess out of him when the door bursts open, banging against the wall. A beaker on the shelf crashes to the ground.

We all look up at once. We don't get many visitors during chess club. Especially not this kind.

Boomer Bodbreath fills the doorway, rubbing his hands together like he just discovered Earth's last stash of Kryptonite.

CHAPTER
26

I LOOK AT GRANT. THE GRIN IS GONE, AND the color has drained from his face.

"Hold it together, man," I whisper. "You can't lose your mojo again."

Boomer swaggers in and scans the room like it's a sold-out stadium and we're his adoring fans. A group of his teammates slouch in the doorway, watching while he walks up and down the aisles, swinging his helmet back and forth by its chin strap.

He stops in front of Dolores and slams the helmet down on her desk. Chess pieces jump off the table, as if they're abandoning ship.

"Game's over, geeks," he snarls.

Dolores doesn't look up. "What do you want, Boomer?"

Boomer grabs a chair and flips it around backward,

plunking himself onto it. He rests his elbows on the back and stares at her, hard.

"You want to know what I want?" He glances at Simon, who wiggles around like someone dropped a handful of ants down his pants. "I want to know which idiot pulled the stunt that got me suspended for three days."

I keep my eyes on the chessboard.

Dolores stands up so fast, her braid smacks her in the face. "You and your friends don't belong here," she scolds. "Why don't you go scramble your brains on the football field?"

Boomer crosses his hands over his heart. "That hurts, you know? I just want someone to fess up so we can make sure there's no hard feelings." He reaches over and clamps his hand down on Simon's bony shoulder. His voice drops at least an octave. "You know anything about that, Booger Boy?"

Even though Simon hasn't eaten his boogers since fourth grade, some nicknames just stick. Booger Boy is one of them.

"No . . . I know nothing. I p-promise," Simon stammers.

Boomer glares at him, his eyes tiny slits. "Well, until someone wants to talk, maybe you'd like to come outside with us." He slides off the chair, looking over at the goons in the doorway. One of them rubs his hands together like Boomer's about to offer him a steak sandwich. "Whaddya say, guys? Should we take Boogie here out for some tackle practice?"

Any second now and Simon's going to hurl his lunch all over Dolores's perfectly pressed skirt. I think about grabbing my journal but change my mind. If Boomer catches me writing an adventure about him, he'll realize his suspicions were right and I am the guy responsible for his suspension. And then I'll be the one hurling all over someone.

"Get your hands off him."

I look up. Grant's standing next to his chair.

"Grant," I whisper. "What the heck are you doing?"

Boomer looks over at us. "You talking to me, four-eyes?" A sneer slides across his face.

"Yeah, I'm talking to you." He cups his ear with his hand. "You need a hearing aid, Bodbreath?"

Oh no. Not again. "Don't do this," I hiss, grabbing the bottom of Grant's T-shirt.

Grant shakes me off him. "Somebody has to do something, Burger."

Boomer lets go of Simon. He glances at the goons in the doorway again.

"You guys take care of Booger Boy. I'll deal with four-eyes."

He starts toward us as his teammates zero in on Simon. One of them cracks his knuckles.

I reach into my backpack, my fingers finding my journal.

Before Grant ends up someplace worse than his locker, or Simon's lunch ends up on his sneakers, I better start writing.

November 5

Episode 7: Bloogfer Returns

Bloogfer zeroed in.

"I told you not to come back here," Dude growled. The Exterminizer was ready. "You've made your last mistake."

Ka-bam! Right on target. The shot was dead-on as Dude dialed the Exterminizer up to MAXIMUM and a stream of purple goo shot straight into Bloogfer's chest.

"I can't...move! My arms...legs...!" His eyes darted back and forth. "I can't move my neck!"

Three more cretins came into Dude's view.

Bam! Bam! Bam! Soon they were all coated in the same purple goo as Bloogfer.

"Explodius, what have you done?" Bloogfer squeezed out. "You've destroyed us!"

"You've destroyed yourself, Bloogfer. Now stop moving, or the toxins will start to eat your flesh

CHAPTER
27

"GIVE ME THAT."

Too late. Before I can finish the sentence, a hand wraps around the back of my neck, and the smell of Simon's tuna sandwich fills the room.

The hand squeezes hard, making my eyes water. Another one grabs my journal.

"Hey!" I yell, but it's no use. Number 32 has me out of my chair and in the air before I know what's happening.

"Whatcha got there?" Boomer growls.

"Little guy is writing something down," Number 32 says, holding my journal up in the air with his other hand. "You want to see it?"

"Throw it over," says Boomer. My journal goes sailing through the air.

I squeeze my eyes closed, waiting for the goose bumps to explode on my skin.

They don't.

I squeeze tighter, trying to see Dude's face.

Nothing.

Great time for a vacation, Dude.

Boomer starts flipping through my journal. If he reads the stuff I've written, he's going to rearrange my face in such a way that even my mom won't recognize me.

Come on, Dude.

I look over at Grant. A guy with spiky hair has shoved him facedown on the chessboard, his arm jerked so far up his back, he can probably scratch his own head. His glasses are twisted sideways, and a pawn is sticking out of his right ear.

I squeeze my eyes closed again. *Concentrate,* I tell myself.

But it's not working. I didn't write enough. We're dead meat.

Just then, a shrieking noise pierces through the room.

"What the—" Number 32 drops me like I'm radioactive and slams his hands over his ears.

The fire alarm.

"Fire!" I scream. "The building's on fire!" Number 32 looks at me like I just suggested he put on a tutu.

"Get out, you big oaf!" I shove him, my hands sinking into his doughy middle. Boomer tosses my journal onto the floor, then stumbles after Number 32 and the rest of his goons. They bump against one another, cursing and yelling the whole way. Finally, they squeeze out and take off toward the exit at the end of the hall.

"Let's go!" I holler, turning back to the others.

Nobody moves except Grant, who sits up and pulls the pawn out of his ear.

"Everyone, line up, single file!"

The chess club gathers around me, waiting. For a second I'm confused, until I realize what's happening—everyone is following my directions.

"Exit's to the right, people. Stay calm, and move in an orderly fashion." Suddenly, I sound a lot like my mom. One after another, everyone files out, first the girls, then Simon, and finally Grant. We make it to the door at the end of the hall, and I shove it open. The sun's so bright, it makes me blink.

"Everyone, come on!" We run out of the building just as we hear the wails of a fire truck.

I rub my eyes and look around. Boomer and his cronies lean against the fence, panting like they've just run a marathon. The chess team is sprawled out on the hill next to me—Grant, Simon, the two seventh-grade girls . . .

Dolores. Where's Dolores?

I tear back toward the exit door and reach it just as three firefighters come jogging around the corner. They break into a run as soon as they see me.

"Oh no, you don't." The first guy slams his hand against the door while another one grabs me up in a bear hug.

"Someone's still in there!" I holler. "And I've got to get her out!" I thrash my legs back and forth, but it's no use. This guy's built like a tree trunk.

"If someone's still in there, we'll find them," he says calmly as the other two guys go into the building. "No need to be a hero, son."

I start to argue but freeze when I see what's coming at me. My mom marches up the sidewalk, her face set like stone.

CHAPTER 28

"WHAT DO YOU THINK YOU'RE DOING?" SHE demands.

The tree trunk spins around. "Huh? Oh, Officer Burger. Had a fire alarm go off inside the school. We're thinking some kid pulled a prank, but Billy and Chet are checking it out now."

Her eyes blaze. "Doug, let go of my son."

"Wha—oh! This your kid?" He lets go of me, and I topple to the ground. "Quite the Good Samaritan, this guy."

She bends down and brushes the hair out of my eyes. "You okay, Charlie? I just heard the call over the radio. . . ."

I scramble to my feet. "I'm fine," I say, pushing her hand away. The tree trunk rocks back on his heels, grinning.

The door opens, and one of the firefighters pokes his head

out. "All clear, Doug. Definitely a prank. We're going to search the building."

Doug gives him a thumbs-up, then looks down at me.

"Not a smart prank. Pulling an alarm when there's no fire can get you into a lot of trouble."

He nods at my mom, then slips inside. I start to turn back to my friends.

"Come with me," my mom says, grabbing my arm.

"Mom, could you not do that here?" I say, looking around to see if anyone's watching us.

She grips harder. "What do you know about this?" she demands.

I look at her like she's lost her marbles. "Nothing. I was at chess club. The fire alarm went off, and I cleared everyone out."

Pulling a pad of paper from her back pocket, she points a finger at me.

"Stay here while I question the others. I mean it, Charlie. Don't move."

Right then, another squad car pulls up. We both look as Officer Gargotti opens the door and hoists himself out. When he sees my mom, a frown the size of Alaska spreads across his face.

"Hey, Gargotti," she calls out, waving. "Sounds like some kids were just messing around. Don't worry; I've got it covered."

"You're off duty," he says, puffing up to us. "You're not even supposed to be here."

"Joe, this is my kids' school."

He crosses his arms, and I can see his undershirt peeking through the gaps in his uniform. "Come on, Betty, don't do this. Chief's already warned you about—"

She puts her hands up, cutting him off. "All right, I get it." She turns and motions for me to follow.

"I'm going to stick around for a little while," I tell her. "I'll meet you at home."

She looks at me like I'm the one missing some marbles. "You'll do no such thing," she says. "Let's go." She looks back at Officer Gargotti. "You know where to find me if you need anything."

We drive home in silence. I keep my eyes focused out the window, watching the clouds that continue to roll in. The radio announcer tells us there's a good-size storm moving in off the Atlantic.

We pull into the driveway, and she cuts the engine. "Charlie," she says. "Please tell me you had nothing to do with whatever went on today at that school."

She can't be serious. "Mom, I already told you. I would never do something like pull a fire alarm."

"Okay, okay. I just wanted to make sure." She gives me a weak smile. "You just never know these days."

Suddenly, my insides are seething. "Yes, you do know! I may not be a star soccer player like Lucy, or Miss Perfect like Stella, but I'm not an idiot."

She looks at me like I just sucker-punched her. "Charles. Of course you're not an—"

"But you're always treating me like one!" I'm yelling now, and my nose is starting to run. "You're always looking over my shoulder, checking my toenails, criticizing my clothes, waiting for me to do something stupid, to mess up." I wipe my face with my sleeve. "You tell me you want me to grow up, but how can I when you're always treating me like I'm a little kid, like today."

"Like today?" Her voice sounds hurt, but I don't care.

"Yes! Like today! Showing up at my school, acting like you have to rescue me, then treating me like I'm some sort of criminal." I blink fast. "It's embarrassing."

We sit there for a minute, me wiping my nose, and her staring off into space. Finally, she speaks, her voice calm. "I'm sorry if I embarrass you, Charlie. But I am your mom. And my first job, above all others, is to protect you." She reaches for my hand. "And even if you don't like it, that's never going to change."

I pull my hand away. "Everything changes, Mom. Everything."

I push the door open and jump out, the tears stinging my eyes as I run.

■ ■ ■

Hours later, I wake up. My room has grown dark, and it's cold—colder than normal. I sit up, thinking I should grab another blanket or maybe go downstairs to see if my dad saved some dinner for me.

And then I hear it.

Something is standing next to me, its breathing raspy and wet.

"I know karate," I whisper. "And my mom has a gun."

Then it lets out a noise, like a howl.

"Owwowwowwoooowwww . . ."

"Lucy? Is that you?" I reach forward and snap on the light. She leans against the edge of my bed, her tongue hanging out. "What are you doing in here? You almost gave me a heart attack."

She howls again so loud that I throw my hand over her mouth.

"You want to wake the whole neighborhood?" I ask her, trying to ignore her wet tongue against my palm. Suddenly, a sharp pain shoots through my hand. It takes me a second to realize she's sunk her teeth into my middle finger. I stuff my other fist in my mouth, trying not to scream.

"Get out!" I screech, and yank my hand free.

Lucy scratches herself for a minute, then scampers out of my room and down the hall.

I sit back against my pillows, sucking on my throbbing finger.

Lucy may be a bratty sister, but this dog thing has gone too far.

I've got to figure out how to switch her back, but how?

I look around for my backpack.

I search under my coat, a towel, and even under my bed.

And then it hits me.

The last time I saw my backpack, it was under my chair during chess club.

The last time I saw my journal, Boomer was tossing it onto the science lab floor.

I've got to get that journal back. And fast.

CHAPTER

29

ON FRIDAY, I GET UP EARLIER THAN USUAL and dress quickly. My plan is simple: I'll go straight to the science room, grab my journal, and write an adventure that will turn Lucy normal again by dinnertime. . . . Well, at least normal for her.

But when I round the corner into the kitchen, my mom and dad are both already at the table. My dad is busy at the stove, and my mom's reading the paper. They both look up when I walk in.

"Dad," I say, still sore at my mom from yesterday, "I'm just going to grab a banana and head out. I've got a lab that I need to finish and—"

He puts up his hands.

"Not so fast, buddy."

"But, Dad . . ."

"Look out the window."

I walk over to the back door and peek through the blinds. The backyard is blanketed in fresh fluffy snow. There's not a lot, but more is falling from the sky.

"Snow day!" He holds up his spatula in a victory salute.

Lucy bounces into the kitchen and scampers to the door. She puts her hands on the glass and presses her nose against it. She lets out a bark.

My mom looks at my dad. "Do you think I should cancel Lucy's appointment with Dr. Daniels today? I really don't want to, but the roads may be dangerous."

My dad sets a plate of pancakes in front of me. "I wouldn't yet. I'm pretty sure the weather forecasters overpredicted this one. Last night they were calling for six inches, but it's too early for that much snow. Now they're saying it'll melt before noon."

I stuff half a pancake in my mouth. "Then I better get to Grant's." Grant's house is right next to the best sledding hill on all of Cape Ann. Plus, I have to pass right by Gatehouse to get there. A quick pit stop to pick up my journal, then—

"First, breakfast," my dad says, pointing to my plate. "Then Grant's."

I cram in another forkful as my mom's cell phone rings. She picks it up immediately.

"Chief? Oh, finally," she says, turning away from the table.

"Thanks for calling me back." She puts her hand around the phone and lowers her voice. "Are you at the middle school now? Great," she says, checking her watch. "I can be there in five minutes." The corners of her mouth turn down. "But, Chief, I really think I should be involved in—" Her head bobs. "Sure, I understand. I'll wait for you at the precinct."

"Any news?" my dad asks.

She shoots him her not-in-front-of-the-children look. "Not yet."

Suddenly, my mouthful of pancake seems harder to swallow than it did a minute ago.

"I'm going down to the station," she says, folding the paper in half. She walks over to the trash can and stuffs the paper inside. "I'll be back in time to take Lucy to her appointment."

She heads for the hallway and motions for my dad to follow. As soon as they're gone, I jump up and run to the trash can. My dad is the king of recycling and would never stand back and watch my mom throw paper away. There's something in there they don't want me to see.

I grab the paper out of the trash and wipe the coffee grounds off the back. I spread it out on the table, peeking around the corner. I can see my dad nodding at something my mom is saying.

"Ruff!" says Lucy.

I point my finger at her. "No barking," I say, and for some reason it works. She starts licking the syrup bottle instead.

I quickly scan the front page but find nothing about Gate-house. I flip it open and look at page two, then three. Not a single mention until the last page.

There, in the bottom left corner, is the headline, *False Fire Alarm at Middle School Suspends One, Four Hospitalized*. I glance up at the back of my dad's head, which is still nodding. I start reading.

A sixth-grade female honors student at Gatehouse Middle School has been suspended for three days after tampering with the fire alarm yesterday afternoon. The incident led to the dispatch of the Cape Ann Fire Department and Cape Ann Police Force. Though no damage was reported and no arrests made, four eighth-grade males have been hospitalized following the incident. An investigation is underway.

I read it again.

A sixth-grade female honors student . . .

Was it Dolores? No, that's crazy. She'd never pull a fire alarm. But she was the only one missing yesterday, and she definitely qualifies as an "honors student." And what about the eighth-grade males? Could they be talking about Boomer and his buffoons? Did something happen to put them in the hospital?

I think about yesterday, and suddenly the words I wrote in my journal come back to me.

The toxins will eat your flesh . . .

Did *I* put those guys in the hospital?

I stuff the paper back in the trash can right as my dad walks into the kitchen again.

"Ready for a couple more pancakes?"

I glance over at Lucy, her hair sticking to her face. "I don't think so," I tell him, heading toward the stairs. "I've got to take care of something first."

CHAPTER

30

I BEG. I PLEAD. I TRY TO STRIKE A DEAL.

"I'll be in and out of the school in less than ten minutes, Mom."

"No, Charlie." She crosses her arms. "And that's final."

When I went upstairs to get dressed, I could see from my bedroom window that the snow wasn't even sticking to the road. I figured I could bike to Gatehouse, grab my journal, and be home before anyone even noticed I was gone. Sledding at Grant's was clearly out.

But when I came back downstairs, my mom was standing in the hallway, pulling a black stocking cap onto her head.

"I forgot my hat," she explained. "It's freezing outside."

Now, standing in front of her, I hold my hands together like I'm praying. "Please, Mom, look," I tell her, unzipping my jacket. "I even put on two sweaters. I planned ahead, see?"

"You are not biking to that school, Charlie. Or anywhere, for that matter."

"I need my science journal, Mom."

She shakes her head. "The homework can wait."

"But—"

She sighs. "Charlie, even if I said yes, it wouldn't matter. The school is locked."

"There must be a janitor or—"

"Charles, you don't understand."

"Understand what, Mom?" Now I cross my arms too. "How can I understand if you don't tell me what's going on?"

She hooks her thumbs into her belt loops, then looks around like she's about to let me in on a national secret.

"Four students from Gatehouse were hospitalized last night. No one knows exactly why, but the doctors have reason to believe they may have contracted meningococcal meningitis."

"Meni-what?"

"Meningococcal meningitis. It's a bacterial infection that can spread quite easily among people who have had close contact with one another." She plays with the clip on her belt. "If left untreated, it can make a person very sick—in some cases it's even fatal."

"Fatal? As in, dead?"

She nods.

"But how do they know that's what they have?" I ask her. "I mean, it could be lots of things, right?"

She bites at her thumbnail. "All four boys showed up in the emergency room last night with rashes that are very specific to this particular infection. Until the tests come back, the kids will stay in the hospital, and the school will remain closed. We don't want an outbreak on our hands."

I feel like someone just punched me in the gut. "The rash . . . Do you know what it looks like?"

She gives me a strange look. "Why?" She reaches for the bottom of my sweater. "Are you showing signs of—"

"I'm fine, Mom," I tell her, moving out of her reach. "I was just curious is all."

She pulls her hat lower and reaches for the door handle. "Well, I'll know more after I go to the precinct." She starts to open the door but then turns back to me. "Promise me you won't go anywhere near Gatehouse or any of your classmates until we have more information."

"But, Mom . . ."

"Meningococcal meningitis is not something to mess with. If you are found anywhere near that school, you will be quarantined until those tests come back, do you understand?"

I nod. "I understand."

"Thank you, Charlie." Her eyes soften. "What you said yesterday in the car about not being a little kid anymore . . . You're right. You are growing up. And I'm proud of you."

She walks out the door. My feet feel like bricks as I turn and drag them back up the stairs, which seem steeper than they did before.

Back in my room, I sit down at my computer and type. Right away, results pop up on to the screen.

Meningococcal meningitis is an aggressive infection that attacks the lining of the brain. Even with rapid identification and treatment, it can cause death.

I scroll farther until I get to the list of symptoms: high fever, neck stiffness, pain in different joints . . .

I stop, and my eyes wander back up. *Neck stiffness?* I think back to the journal entry. After Bloogfer got shot with the Exterminizer, didn't he say he couldn't move his neck?

I keep reading until I find what I'm looking for. It's even typed in bold.

A red or purple skin rash *may indicate blood poisoning, in which case you should seek medical attention immediately.*

My whole body starts to shake. The goo that Dude shot at Boomer and the others was purple.

Did Dude give those guys this disease?

Are they going to die because of me?

■ ■ ■

Pickles picks up on the first ring.

"Yeah?" She says it fast, like she was expecting my call.

"Pickles, it's me, Charlie."

"Did you work everything out?"

I push my door closed with my foot. "Just the opposite," I say, my voice cracking. "I've made a mess of everything."

"Tell me," she says.

So I do. I tell her about Dude and turning Lucy into a dog, and the dance, and how Mr. P thinks I might be something called a bully buster. I tell her about Coach losing his voice and our winning the game. And then I tell her about chess club and the fire alarm and how my journal is gone and the school is closed and how Boomer and his friends might have meningococcal meningitis and if they die, it's because of me.

She clears her throat. "Meni-what?"

"Meni—oh, never mind. That's not important. What's important is, I've got to figure out how to get my journal and fix the mess I've made. I just want everything to go back to the way it was. I want everything to be normal again."

"Slow down," she says. "First of all, how do you know those kids in the hospital are the same bozos who showed up at your chess club?"

I think about this for a minute. Maybe she's right. . . . Maybe it's all just a coincidence. The paper said it was four eighth-grade males, but that was all. There are lots of eighth-grade males at Gatehouse. And, even if it is Boomer and his bozos, maybe their infection has nothing to do with me. The article I read said the rash could be red or purple. Until I know more details, this could have nothing at all to do with Dude Explodius or his last adventure.

"I've got to go to the hospital, Pickles," I say. "I've got to see if it's Boomer, and if it is, if his rash is purple."

"And if it is?"

"Then I've got to find that journal and fix this. Before it's too late."

I hear a chime in the background, signaling a customer coming into the store. "I've got to go, Charlie," she says, her voice low. "If you need me . . ."

"Pickles?"

"Yeah?"

I grip the phone tighter. "Do you think Gramps was a bully buster?"

For a minute, she doesn't say anything. When she finally does, her voice is heavy.

"I don't know, Charlie. Like I told you before, I didn't understand a lot of what he was doing in that lab, and to be honest, I didn't ask a lot of questions. But I know one thing for sure."

"What's that?"

"He wanted to make a difference." She sighs. "And he was willing to risk everything to make that happen."

I hang up, knowing what I have to do.

■ ■ ■

Twenty minutes later, I'm leaning my bike against a RESERVED FOR PHYSICIANS ONLY sign and staring across the parking lot at Cape Ann Medical Center. Even though most of the snow has already melted, patches of it linger on the grass and bushes around me.

I look down at the watch I grabbed off my dad's dresser. I feel bad that I lied to him, but it was the only way he'd let me leave the house without making a stink about it.

"Dad, I'm going to Anthony's!" I hollered, heading down the stairs and scooting toward the front door.

"Anthony Gargotti?" He wandered out of the kitchen, holding a plate of homemade muffins. "I thought your mom told you to stay put."

I was prepared for him to say something like this. "She said I had to stay away from anyone who goes to Gatehouse. Anthony goes to a different school, remember?"

He handed me a muffin. "I don't know, Charlie. Anthony is . . ."

I was prepared for this, too. "Come on, Dad. We're just going to play video games, not steal a car."

He laughed at that, and then said fine, I could go, as long as I was home before dinner and didn't try any funny business. Now, staring up at the hospital, I can't think of anything less funny than what I'm about to do.

A gust of cold air smacks me in the face. "Stop being a

baby, Burger," I mutter, and hurry across the sidewalk and into the building. "You can do this. You can."

The lobby is glossy and white and reminds me of last winter when my dad and I brought Franki here after she'd fallen while skating at Mill Pond. She had to wear a cast up to her elbow for six weeks, but it smelled like foot fungus after four.

Thinking about Franki makes me feel better. I wish she could have seen the way I handled things yesterday after the fire alarm went off. Maybe she would have finally realized I did have guts. A lot of them, in fact.

I walk across the white tiles to a desk that sits smack in the middle of the room. An INFORMATION sign hangs above it. A woman watches as I approach, but she doesn't move the cell phone from her ear.

"You just wouldn't believe what's going on, Eugene," she's saying into the phone. "The switchboard lit up as soon as the paper came out this morning, reporters wanting updates and parents wondering if their own children need to be tested. What? Have I seen them?" She rolls her eyes like this is the craziest thing ever. "Honey, I didn't fall off the turnip truck yesterday. Until they figure out what's wrong with those boys, I'm not stepping foot anywhere near the third floor." She lowers her voice a little. "From what I hear, they're not doing too good."

My insides flip over. I cough, hoping that will get her attention. I don't cover my mouth.

"I've got to go," she says. "Yes, I'll call. The second I know more . . ." She turns off the phone, drops it into a bag on the floor, and then swivels around to her computer.

"Name?" she says to the screen.

"Charlie."

She inspects a long fingernail, then another. Finally, she looks up at me, her eyelids heavy.

"Of the patient."

"Oh—uh . . ." I think for a second but realize I don't even know what Boomer's real name is. Nobody would actually name their kid Boomer, would they?

"Bodbreath. I'm wondering if Mr. Bodbreath is here."

Her fingers quit typing.

"Only immediate family members are allowed in the quarantine area."

A chill runs down my spine. So, he *is* here. "Well, I am," I say, thinking fast. "An immediate family member, that is."

She narrows her eyes at me.

"We're cousins. Close cousins." I cross my fingers. "We're like this. Tight."

"Of course you are," she says, holding out her hand. "I just need to see your identification and then I'll call security."

"Security?"

She points to a pile of bright-orange badges that sit on her desk. CLEARED FOR VISITATION is stamped across the front of each one. "Security must sign off before I can give you one of those." She glares at me. "It's the only way you're getting to the third floor."

We stare at each other for a minute, neither of us backing down. Finally, I reach into my back pocket, pretending to dig for my wallet. A light on the switchboard starts blinking.

She points a skinny finger at me. "Don't move."

Right away, her voice changes. "Cape Ann Medical Center," she singsongs. "How may I—" Her eyes double in size. "Channel Three News!" Swiveling away from me, she pats her hair. "An interview?" She giggles like a schoolgirl. "Well, sure. I'd be more than happy to . . . Yes, I'll hold."

Bending over, she starts to rifle through her bag, and I see my chance. Reaching down, I snag one of the security passes off her desk. The bank of elevators is in front of me, and I make a run for it. As the doors slide open, I look back.

Cradling the hospital phone on one ear, she holds her cell phone up to the other. "Oh, Eugene!" I can hear her say. "You will not believe this! Guess who's going to be on the five-o'clock news!"

Seconds later, I step out onto the third floor. A nurses' station is in front of me. Two women sit behind it, their heads bent down. Next to them, a machine lets out tiny beeps.

"May I help you?"

I practically jump out of my skin. I look up and see a tiny woman, dressed in white, standing next to me.

"Uh . . ." Now I have to pee. Maybe I should rethink my

plan. Isn't it enough that I know he's here? Do I have to see him, too?

I shoot what I hope is a convincing smile at the lady. "Wrong floor," I say, turning around and jabbing the down button on the wall. The doors slide open, and I step on, relieved.

"Wait!" She points at the orange pass that I'm holding. "You must be here to see one of the boys."

"I . . . Well, yeah, kind of . . ." I sound like an idiot.

"I'm Nurse Amy," she says, grabbing my hand. She pulls me off the elevator. "And you don't have to be scared. With the proper protection, you'll be fine."

I hope you know what you're talking about, lady, I think as I stumble down the hall behind her.

We make our way down a long corridor. At the end, we come to another set of double doors with a sign above them that reads: QUARANTINE AREA. AUTHORIZED PERSONS ONLY.

"You need to slip this on," she says, grabbing a jumpsuit from a cart next to us. "It's for your own protection."

I take it and struggle into something that looks and feels like an oversize garbage bag. When I'm done, she nods at me, then snaps a pair of goggles over my eyes.

"Leave these on, okay?"

"Okay," I say.

"Which one are you here to see?"

"Bodbreath," I say before I can change my mind.

She nods again and pushes a button. The doors swing open.

"He's in there," she says, pointing to a single door on our left. I start to move forward, then stop, looking back at her.

"Go on," she says, smiling. "It's fine."

Fine like walking into a lion's den, I think as I walk over to the door and pull.

■ ■ ■

At first, everything's blurry, and I think about pulling off the goggles, but then I remember what the nurse said. After a few seconds, my eyes start to adjust to the dark, and I look around.

In the far corner, I see the outline of a hospital bed. A panel full of lights hangs on the wall behind it, blinking like a Christmas tree. A faint beeping is the only sound in the room. At the foot of the bed is a small table littered with wads of tissue.

"Hello, there."

I swear, I jump twenty feet. Now I really have to pee.

A dark figure emerges from the corner.

"Thanks for coming."

I blink. The voice is soft and small. I squint through the goggles.

"I am Mrs. Bodbreath," she says, "Sherrel's mother."

I blink again. *"Sherrel?"*

She smiles, and I can see a space where a tooth should be. "I know, I know. He's so embarrassed by his name, always telling me it was meant for a girl. But it's been in my family for many generations. It was my grandfather's."

"Oh," I say, trying to imagine Boomer being embarrassed about anything.

She goes on. "I'm so glad you've come to visit." She presses her lips together. "How did you manage that, anyway? I thought only family was allowed."

I think fast. "Uh . . . my mom's a police officer. She got special permission."

She beams as if this is the best news she's heard all week. "Oh, that's so nice. And what position do you play?"

It takes me a minute to realize she's talking about football. My face gets hot.

"I don't," I say, shaking my head. "Play on the team, that is."

"Oh? Then how do you two know each other?"

"Chess club," I blurt out. I want to shoot myself. Really, I do.

"Chess!" She glances over at the bed. "I bet he's good. He's always been very strategic, you know."

Not exactly a word I'd use to describe Boomer, but I nod anyway.

"Well, you boys will be playing together again before you know it." She says it like she's trying to convince herself as much as anyone else. "Now come say hello."

I hold up a gloved hand.

"Uh, that's okay, Mrs. Bodbreath." I shift my weight from one foot to the other, my bladder about to explode. "I just . . . Can you just tell me . . . The rash. What color is it?"

She doesn't seem to hear me. Instead, she leans over the lump in the bed, cooing. "Peanut," she says, "you have a visitor."

Peanut?

She looks up. "What did you say your name was, dear?"

"Charlie." It comes out before I can stop it. I rack my brain, trying to remember if there is another Charlie at our school. There isn't.

"Charlie's here," she whispers to the lump. "He misses playing chess with you."

Oh jeez . . . If Boomer survives this, I'm so dead.

"Come here, dear," she says, holding her hand out to me. My feet shuffle forward like they're not my own.

I look down. An eerie light radiates from Boomer's skin, as if he's swallowed a pack of purple glow sticks. "Wow," I say, "he's purple, all right."

Mrs. Bodbreath nods. "That's what has the doctors most concerned." She leans toward me, whispering. "They're worried it may be blood poisoning."

I gulp.

"But he's going to be fine," she says, her voice so full of peppiness, it would put my sister's cheerleading squad to shame. "Yes, you are, Peanut. Don't you worry."

Boomer grunts.

"Don't try to move," she says, then looks at me. "His neck is very stiff."

He grunts again.

"I think he's trying to say something," she says. "What is it, Peanut? What are you trying to say?"

It's faint, but it's undeniable. "Charlie," he whispers.

My blood stops moving.

"I think he wants to talk to you," Mrs. Bodbreath says. She pushes me toward the bed. For someone so tiny, she's stronger than she looks.

"Get closer," she demands.

Any closer and I might as well kiss him, I want to say. I can practically count the freckles on his purply skin.

His eyes are buggy, like someone's shoving on them from the inside out. They dart back and forth, searching my face.

"My mom," he mumbles. "She thinks . . . we're . . . friends. . . ."

I nod.

"Friends . . ." His eyes dart around some more. "Get it?"

And suddenly, I do. Boomer Bodbreath might be Gatehouse Middle School's biggest bully, but he still wants his mom to be proud of him.

"What's he saying, Charlie?" Mrs. Bodbreath pokes a bony finger into my back. "Can you understand what he's saying?"

I straighten up but keep my eyes on Boomer's.

"I understand him perfectly."

She closes her eyes. "Oh, thank you." I have a feeling this isn't meant for me.

I wiggle my way out from between the two of them. "I'm sorry, Mrs. Bodbreath, but I really need to go."

"Already?" Her eyes snap open. "But you'll come back, yes?"

I bolt toward the door. "Hopefully, I won't have to."

■ ■ ■

Outside, the sky has grown darker. A few snowflakes are falling again, and I can taste sea salt on my lips. I zip up my jacket and jump onto my bike. I've got to get that journal. I speed across town but screech to a stop when I see Gatehouse. It looms in front of me, looking more like a Hollywood movie set than my middle school. Spotlights blaze in the parking lot, and television vans are parked next to a row of black town cars. Two guards dressed in khaki military duds stand in front of each set of doors, and a man in a dark trench coat paces back and forth, a cell phone stuck to his ear. A reporter pops out of one of the vans, and I grab her before she can go by.

"Hey . . . uh, can you tell me what's going on?" I ask, trying to sound casual.

She gives me a sideways glance.

"Breaking news," she says, the wind pushing her words back in her face. "The CDC just arrived."

"CDC?"

"Center for Disease Control," she says, trying to swipe the hair out of her face. "You should get out of here, kid. If they find you snooping around, they're going to quarantine you until this whole thing is over. Meningococcal meningitis is big news, especially in a small town like this one."

She runs past me, and I stare at Gatehouse. If only I could get inside, I could put a stop to all this. But there are so many people, and there's no—wait, what was that? In the window of Mr. P's science lab, a small yellow light blinks at me. Once, twice . . . then again.

He's in there. Mr. P is back.

I dump my bike next to the streetlight and run across the road. After ducking behind a maple tree, I skirt across the courtyard, trying to stay in the shadows.

I'm almost to the window when I hear voices behind me. I scrunch down behind a bush and try to make myself as small as possible.

"So, you think these kids are really sick?" A thick Boston accent floats over my head, and I look up. Two men dressed in trench coats head up the hill toward Maggie's Coffee Shop.

"Beats me," says the other. "They say they got all the symptoms."

I pop my head up and look around. The light in the window blinks again, and I jump up and grab the sill. As soon as I press my face against the glass, I can see him clear as day.

Mr. P sits in his leather chair, reading. He holds a book in one hand and a coffee mug in the other. His cowboy hat dips forward, most of his face hidden from sight.

That's just great, I think. This place is crawling with reporters and something called the CDC, and my science teacher is sitting in his science lab, sipping cowboy coffee and reading like he doesn't have a care in the world. I'm about to reach out and tap on the glass, when I notice two beady eyes staring at me.

"Ack!" I scream, and fall backward into the bush.

"Charlie?" The top of a cowboy hat leans out the window. "That you, pardner?"

The beady eyes belong to something that is now climbing onto his shoulder. I shudder.

"Is that a rat?" I scramble to stand up.

"What? Oh, you mean Whiz?" He reaches over and plucks it off, holding it out to me. "Want to hold him?"

"No!" I screech, then clamp my hand over my mouth and look around. "What's he doing here?"

"Just keeping me company. Doesn't like to be locked up when there's a ruckus. He's a chinchilla. Part of the rodentia family, similar to his distant cousin, the ground squirrel. These little critters are crepuscular, meaning he's a bundle of energy early in the morning and right around sundown—"

"Mr. P," I interrupt, my teeth chattering. "Can I—"

"Know where they're from?"

I look behind me. "Who?"

"Chinchillas." He doesn't wait for me to answer. "The Andes. In South America. Want me to show you on a map?"

I try again. "Mr. P? Is there any chance—"

"You could come inside? Well, sure thing." He reaches out of the window and grabs ahold of my arms. Before I can argue, he's hoisted me up the bricks and through the window.

I glance around. It could almost pass as our regular science lab. Rows of tables—their stainless-steel tops scrubbed clean—fill the center of the room, six chairs on top of each, like soldiers standing at attention. Beakers and microscopes line the back counters, and the textbooks are stacked neatly against the wall, waiting to be cracked open again. But the leather chair in the corner with the cowhide rug lying next to it throws the whole thing off. And though there's no smell of bacon grease, it's pretty obvious that this room is more than just a science lab to Mr. P.

He jerks his head to the side, motioning toward something on the table next to the leather chair.

"I reckon you've come for that."

My science journal.

"You found it!" I pick it up and hold it to my chest. Goose bumps explode all over me.

"I didn't find it," he says, "It—"

I cut him off. "It found me."

He grins. "Good work, pardner."

"But it's not good, Mr. P. In fact, it's very, very bad. I stink at this bully-busting stuff."

His grin disappears. "Why would you say that?"

I plunk down on the leather chair, my head in my hands. "Because every time I think I've figured it out, something comes along to prove me wrong. I've messed up more things than I've fixed, and I can't make sense of any of it."

He bends down next to me. "Charlie. What was the most important thing I told you on the first day of science class?"

I peek out from between my fingers. "That we should write from our guts?"

He shakes his head.

"That . . . words can be powerful?"

He puts his hand on my knee. "Think."

I squeeze my eyes closed, trying to remember the details of that first day. Showing up late, his cowboy boots click-clacking on the tile floor, the shock I felt when I first touched the journal . . .

My eyes spring open. "You told me that a true scientist will not be satisfied with finding the answers to the things that makes sense. A true scientist will ask questions about the things that don't."

He pulls a toothpick from his pocket and sticks it into his mouth. "Bingo," he says, winking.

"But," I say slowly, "you also told me something else."

"Go on," he says.

Suddenly, the room feels too hot.

"You told me that even after a scientist's got his answers, he won't be satisfied." I stand up. "You're still not satisfied, are you?"

His eyebrows shoot up under the brim of his hat. "What's this have to do with me?"

I think back to what Stella said in the van on the first day of school. "Every year, you hand out a bunch of journals and say all this stuff about magic and power and words, and how everyone should write from the gut. Then you sit back and wait to see who will fall for it." I wipe my brow. "If no one does, you give up, then start from scratch the next year."

"Now, look here, pardner—" he says.

I glare at him. "This whole thing . . . This was your experiment, not mine."

"You're wrong, Charlie." He points his toothpick at me. "You're letting doubt get in the way of your imagination."

"But that's the problem!" My voice is rising. "It's been a figment of my imagination all along. There was no magic or catalyst or special gift—just some dumb kid who wanted to believe that a made-up superhero could change things for the better."

He stares at me. "You really believe that?"

I close my eyes, thinking back over everything that's happened. Lucy turning into a dog, Boomer stripping naked,

Coach losing his voice . . . Did my words really have the power to make these things happen?

"Believe what you want, Charlie," Mr. P says softly. He points at my chest. "But the power to change things lives in there. How you get it out is up to you."

"Was my grandfather one of your experiments, too?"

He looks at me like I just punched him. "Your grandfather believed that anything was possible."

My voice cracks. "But he died because of it."

Suddenly, there's another voice, from the hallway.

"Charles? Is that you?"

I look around, frantic. "It's my mom! If she finds me . . ."

"Charlie? Are you in there?"

The footsteps stop right outside the door. Mr. P stands in the middle of the room, stroking his dumb rodent, looking through the door, not at it. He's gone somewhere else, far away from Gatehouse and the science lab.

The handle turns, and I nose-dive under the closest table.

I hear a creak and the all-too-familiar sound of heavy police boots filling the room. Closer and closer they clomp until they stop right in front of my nose.

Please, I think, squeezing my eyes closed tight, *please don't see me.*

I lie like that for what feels like forever. Finally, I peel open my left eyelid and squint out.

Her face is less than a millimeter from mine.

"Ack!" I say for the second time today.

"Don't. Say. Anything." Her eyelashes brush against my cheek, and her black stocking cap is pulled so low on her forehead, she looks more like a ninja than a mom.

"Look . . . I can explain."

She grabs ahold of my shirtsleeves and slides me out from under the table like I'm a sack of dirty laundry. I drop the journal as she hauls me over to the open window and plunks me down on the ledge.

"Mom." I look back over her shoulder. My journal lies in the middle of the floor, just inches from her boot. Catalyst or not, I can't leave it behind. "I know you're mad, but I just need to grab—"

Her words send a chill through me. "You defied me. I told you not to come here, and you did anyway."

I try again. "But I had no choice. So, if you'll just reach down and—"

"You had a choice, Charlie. You just made the wrong one."

She shoves me off the ledge, and for a second I'm free-falling, my arms and legs like pinwheels in the air. I land in the bush, a blanket of snow puffing out around me.

"Mom! What'd you do that for?" I scramble out, glaring up at her.

She leans out the window, her eyes darting every which

way. "We have to go immediately. You are not supposed to be here. I am not supposed to be here. If anyone finds us . . ."

We both hear it at the same time. A police siren wailing up Beach Street.

She points in the direction of my bike. "Go. No matter what, don't stop. Do you understand?"

"Aren't you coming?" I ask.

"I'm right behind you," she says, hoisting herself onto the window ledge.

I look around. A reporter is climbing out of a van, signaling at his cameraman to follow. They must have heard the sirens, too.

"Mom," I beg, my voice hoarse. "I need that journal. It's on the floor, right next to—"

"Can't you just do what I'm asking for once?"

I nod, too shocked to say another word.

"Go!"

I take off toward the street. When I get to my bike, I turn.

At first, I can't see her, and I start to worry. After a second, she pops back up, and I see my journal tucked under her arm. She slides onto the windowsill and is getting ready to jump when a squad car pulls up next to her, its blue-and-red lights flashing across her face.

"Police!" I hear someone shout. "Don't move!"

I look around, panicky. Should I go back? She told me to

go home no matter what. I can't disobey her again. I jump onto my bike and pedal down Beach Street, my legs pumping like crazy.

She's a police officer, I keep telling myself. She'll know what to do. She always does.

CHAPTER
31

THAT NIGHT, I DREAM ABOUT FRANKI.

It's summer, and we are walking on Pebble Beach, holding hands like we used to before holding hands mattered. Franki's telling me a joke that's cracking me up. She's smiling and I can barely look at her, she's so bright. But then I realize she's getting brighter and brighter, and pretty soon it's like trying to look directly at the sun. I let go of her hand to shield my eyes, and before I know it she's gone.

"Franki! Come back!"

I wake up clawing at my eyes, only to realize I forgot to close my shades. The sun shines through my window, yesterday's storm long gone.

I sit up, and that's when I smell it.

I breathe deeper. Maybe I'm still dreaming.

I tiptoe across the wood floor. My feet are like ice cubes, but there's no time to fool with socks.

Not when the smell of bacon—real bacon!—is invading my bedroom.

Before I can make it down the stairs, Lucy appears, her lips pulled back in a snarl.

"I'm so not in the mood," I tell her.

She grabs a mouthful of my pajama leg and pulls, almost knocking me off-balance.

"Sit!" I command, and she does.

I study her face. There's something about the way she looks at me that I hadn't noticed before, almost like she's trying to tell me something. "What is it, Lucy?" I say, bending down. "Is this all just a figment of my imagination?" I lean closer. "Or did I really turn you into a dog?"

"Gaaaah!" I scream as her tongue slides across my lips, coating me in half an inch of saliva. I jump backward, and she lunges for my pant leg again, but this time I'm too quick. I race out of the room, wiping my mouth with the back of my hand.

I look down at my knuckles, strands of my sister's slobber hanging off them.

This is definitely not a figment of my imagination.

■ ■ ■

Downstairs, the smell of bacon grows stronger, and I feel like I've won the lottery, a trip to Disneyland, and the district championship all in one.

I follow it into the kitchen.

My dad stands next to the stove, holding a spatula in one hand and a cup of coffee in the other. His BURGER'S BEST VEGGIE BURGER apron covers his pajama pants. He turns when he hears me walk in.

"Ready for breakfast?" he asks. I nod and plunk down at the table, glad he still hasn't brought up yesterday.

After I'd left Gatehouse, I made it home in record time. When I got to the house, Stella told me that Dad had taken Lucy to her shrink appointment, since Mom had called and said she was still tied up at the precinct. I grabbed a bag of Mom's hidden Doritos and headed straight to my room, knowing I'd be in for a major lecture later.

But the lecture never came. When my dad called us all for dinner, my mom still wasn't home, and he was too distracted to ask me about my day.

"Mom on her way?" I asked, looking at my plate. I was so full of Doritos, it was hard to even pretend like I was hungry.

"Still at the precinct," my dad said, dumping a spoonful of rice pilaf onto the middle of my plate. "Busy day, I guess."

I felt bad not telling him what had happened, but I figured it was better to let my mom fill him in. Plus, if I was going to get yelled at, I'd rather get yelled at only once.

Now, my stomach rumbles and I realize I'm starving. "Smells great, Dad," I say as he sets a plate of bacon and eggs in front of me. "I can't believe you cooked bacon!"

"I didn't," he says, pointing his spatula toward the hallway. "She did."

As if on cue, Pickles rounds the corner, a cup of coffee in one hand and an unlit cigar in the other.

"Pickles!" I run to her like I'm five again. "What are you doing here?" I ask.

She looks at my dad.

"Come back here, son," he says, walking over to the table and sitting down. He pats my chair.

I do as I'm told. Pickles sits down, too. My dad clears his throat. "Charlie, your mom didn't come home last night."

Suddenly, the room feels like someone sucked all the air out of it.

"She's okay, right?" I look from him to Pickles, then back again.

Pickles nods. "She's fine." She raises an eyebrow at my dad.

He fiddles with the saltshaker in front of him. "Yesterday, while you were at the Gargottis', your mom called and asked me to take Lucy to her doctor's appointment because she was tied up with work. She also asked to speak with you."

Uh-oh.

He continues. "I tried to tell her you had gone to Anthony's, but she wasn't buying it. I even offered to call over there just to make sure, but she hung up before I could even finish my sentence. It wasn't until later that I found out she went to Gatehouse, looking for you."

I pick at a stain on my T-shirt. I can feel my dad's eyes on me.

"By the way, I never did call the Gargottis," he says softly, "because I knew you wouldn't lie to me."

There's a lump in my throat the size of a watermelon. "Where is she now?" I manage to squeeze out.

Pickles sighs. "She's in the clinker."

"The *what?*"

"Jail. She spent the night in jail."

"Jail?"

My dad stands up and starts pacing the kitchen.

"She was found climbing out of a window at Gatehouse," Pickles says. "She was arrested for breaking and entering."

"Breaking and entering?" I'm starting to sound like a parrot.

My dad presses his lips together. "*Alleged* breaking and entering," he says. "No charges have been filed."

I think back to yesterday, watching my mom climb out of the science lab window right as the squad car showed up. "But she can't be arrested," I say, her favorite phrase popping into my head. "She's an officer of the law."

"An *officer* of the law, yes," Pickles says, fiddling with her cigar. "Above the law, no."

I stand up. "She was there because of me."

Pickles stops fiddling and my dad stops pacing. They both look at me.

"She told me not to go there. But I did anyway." The image of her tucking my journal under her arm won't stop running through my head. I look from my dad to Pickles. "They found her there because of me."

We hear a whimper and all turn. Lucy sits in the doorway of the kitchen, one of my mom's slippers in her mouth.

"Lucy," my dad says, going over to her. He bends down. "I didn't know you were there, sweetie."

Pickles turns to me.

"You okay?" she says.

I shake my head and bolt for the back door.

■ ■ ■

It's Pickles who finds me.

"Thought you might be down here," she says, walking up behind me. She's breathing heavier than she does normally. "You probably didn't know this, but your grandfather liked the beach, too. Said it was a good place to let his ideas run around a bit."

I'm sitting cross-legged on a piece of driftwood on the edge of the sand. Even though the snow has melted, I can feel the wetness of the wood soaking through the bottom of my pajama pants.

Pickles plunks down next to me, pulling her jacket around her.

"It's my fault, Pickles," I tell her. "I've made a mess of everything."

"I know, Charlie."

I glance over at her. "Gee, thanks for making me feel better."

She grunts a little as she pulls her legs up closer to her chest. "But that's what it's all about, isn't it?"

"What do you mean?"

She stares out toward the water like she's looking for someone.

"You ever hear of a guy named Alexander Fleming?"

I shake my head.

"Well, Fleming was a scientist who loved spending time in his lab, but he was very messy. One day, he was getting ready to leave for a vacation, but he didn't have time to clean up after his latest experiment, so he just left all his equipment out. When he returned, he discovered something growing in the dishes, something amazing—something that would change the world of medicine forever."

I sit forward. "What was it?"

"Penicillin. Those unwashed dishes grew a type of mold that was later turned into something that would save lives in a way no medicine had before. And all because Fleming hadn't had time to clean up his mess."

She looks at me out of the corner of her eye. "Sometimes, we have to make a bit of a mess to see something differently."

She reaches inside her coat and pulls out my journal.

"Your mom gave it to me this morning when I went to see her." She smiles at me. "She said you needed it."

I look down at it. "I don't know what to believe anymore, Pickles."

"Your grandfather believed anything was possible," she says, struggling to her feet. "But at some point you have to start believing in yourself. That's all any of us can do."

∎ ∎ ∎

When we get back to the house, my dad is trying to convince Lucy that it's too cold to go outside and that if she doesn't quit scratching the back door, she's going to have to repaint it herself. Pickles jumps in to help, and I sneak past and head to my room.

I sit down at my desk and look at the journal. Running my hand over the cover, I think about that first day of class when Mr. P handed it to me and told me to write stuff instead of recording science experiments. Now I know he was conducting an experiment of his own.

Maybe it's time I conduct my own, too.

I flip back through the journal, reading over the things I wrote. Mr. P had said that a bully buster has the power to change things for the better, but it seems like I've changed a lot of things for the worse. Words can be powerful, all right, but that power can be good or bad, depending on how you use it.

Believe in yourself, Pickles had said.

Had that been Gramps's problem? Had he believed in his journal more than he had himself?

I flip to a blank page. Maybe it's time to stop believing in superheroes, and just believe in me.

Maybe it really is time to grow up.

I pick up my pencil.

I don't know if it's the right choice, but it's my choice.

I start writing.

November 7
Episode 8: Dude's Final Adventure

Staring out over the vast planet, Dude knew it
was time. His rule had been successful, and the
people now lived in peace. Bloogfer and Croach had
found their places among the inhabitants of Planet
Splodii, and their reign of terror had come to an
end. Planet Splodii no longer needed a superhero.
    His work was done.
    He called for Bill. The dog leaped toward him,
licking his chops after having finished his final meal:
three T-bone steaks, rare, and a pint of Double-
Mocha Monster Crunch ice cream. Wagging his tail,
Bill came and stood by his master.
    Dude shape shifted his arm into the Exterminizer
and pointed it at the dog. He turned the dial to
DISABLE, then pulled the trigger.
    <u>Whoosh!</u> Within seconds, a fog filled the air,
surrounding Bill. As the air cleared, the Imbecile
stood in the spot where the dog had been.
    "Behave yourself," he told her, "or I'm coming
back for you."
    Then he turned the dial to DISASSEMBLE and
pointed it at himself. He looked down the mountain
at the people below.

"Take care of one another," he said, and pulled the trigger again.

Poof! As the citizens of Splodii looked up, they saw a golden cloud fill the air above them, then slowly lift off into space. They bowed their heads in unison.

For many months afterward, people on Splodii would claim that on very clear days, small golden particles could be seen floating through the atmosphere, reminding them of the superstudly guy who had successfully rid their universe of evil.

Dude Explodius was gone.

At least, until someone, somewhere, needed him again.

CHAPTER

32

"DINNER!" I HOLLER WHILE I FOLD THE LAST
napkin. Normally, I make myself scarce when it's time to set
the table. But tonight, it feels good to help.

I think about my decision to get rid of Dude Explodius.
Even though I'm not looking forward to getting chewed out
by Coach or having to keep a low profile around guys like
Boomer, maybe it's worth it just to have things be normal again.

Don't get me wrong. I have nothing against superheroes.
I just don't need to believe I am one.

As I set down the last glass, Pickles and Stella come into
the dining room, Pickles carrying a pan of lasagna, and Stella,
a basket of homemade wheat berry rolls. Everyone looks
around.

"Where's Lucy?" my dad asks, tossing the salad.

"Probably out chasing cars," I say. "Or eating the mailman."

My dad shoots me a look that shuts me up.

"This is getting ridiculous," mutters Pickles. She takes the cigar from her mouth. "Lucille Evelyn Burger!" Her scream makes us wince. "Get yourself down here right now!"

Seconds later, Lucy walks into the room.

The first thing I notice is the bow. Bright pink and wider than my dad's size-eleven work shoes, it perches on top of her head like a tiara. Her curls hang in neat spirals around her shoulders, even more boingy than they were before. And her dress? It's the color of cotton candy and looks like something straight out of one of those princess shows she likes. When she walks by me, I catch a whiff of her strawberry lip gloss.

She's Lucy again.

She pulls out a chair and sits down carefully. Like a surgeon preparing his instruments, she spreads her napkin across her lap and adjusts her knife, fork, and spoon. Finally, she looks up at us.

My dad holds the serving spoon in midair, red sauce dripping onto my mom's favorite tablecloth, while Pickles and Stella seem to have forgotten how to chew. Their mouths hang open, too stunned to say anything.

"What?" Lucy says, looking around the table.

My dad, seeing the sauce, dumps the spoonful of lasagna onto Pickles's plate and wipes up the spill with his finger.

"You look lovely, sweetie," he says.

227

"Totally." Stella nods.

"About time," I mutter, and grab two rolls. I'm hungrier than I've been in weeks.

■ ■ ■

I'm on my third helping of lasagna when the front door creaks open.

We all stop, frozen.

"Hello?" we hear from the front hallway.

"Mommy!" Lucy jumps out of her chair, smacking her plate with her forearm. Half of her salad lands in my lap.

The rest of us get up and follow my sister into the hallway. My mom stands in the open doorway, her face already buried in Lucy's hair. They stand like that for what seems like forever. My mom looks up, her eyes searching my dad's. He shrugs and smiles.

I stare at my mom standing in our front hall, looking tired but happy. I resist the urge to copy Lucy.

"Food's getting cold." Pickles places her hands on Stella's shoulders and steers her back toward the dining room, motioning for the rest of us to follow. "Your mom must be starving, guys," she says over her shoulder. "Let's go fix her a plate."

■ ■ ■

Later, after the dishes are washed and Pickles has beaten me at Battleship twice, I go upstairs to get ready for bed. I'm brushing my teeth when I hear my parents' voices coming from their bedroom on the other side of my bathroom wall.

"I still don't understand why you did it." My dad's voice is tight, like his vocal cords are stretched too thin.

"Because I'm his mother," I hear my mom say. "Who knows what would have happened if someone had found him in there? The panic surrounding those boys' illness has gotten out of control."

I stop moving my toothbrush and listen.

"But the consequences for you—"

"I knew the consequences before I went in there." She sniffs, like her nose is running.

My dad grunts. "I can't believe the chief suspended you for this."

Suspended? From the police force?

"Well, this isn't my first . . . incident. Chief had warned me."

They're both quiet for a minute, then I hear a noise, like someone's crying.

"Come here," my dad says, his voice softening. "It's going to be okay."

"I know." My mom's voice is muffled, like she's talking into his shirt. "I just hate for the kids to see me like this."

"Nobody's perfect," he says. The sobbing grows louder. "Maybe it's time we all come to terms with that."

I turn and spit what's left of my toothpaste into the sink, then climb into my bed.

I'm just about to drift off when my door creaks open, and the light from the hall falls across my bed.

"Charles?"

I keep my eyes closed tight.

"Charlie?" My mom sits down on my bed. "Are you still awake?"

I open one eye.

"Hi," she says, smiling at me.

"This is all my fault, Mom," I tell her. "I lied to you and Dad. On top of that, if I hadn't asked you to get my journal—"

She brushes the hair out of my eyes. "It's not your fault, Charlie. I made my choices. I have to live with them."

I want to say something else, but my eyes won't stay open. I don't know how long she sits there, but I fall asleep like that, her sitting there, watching me.

It's kind of nice, to be honest.

■ ■ ■

"And no death games. They're going to a dance, not war."

I look down at the rows of naked Barbies splayed out on Lucy's bed, and I shake my head.

At their last appointment, Dr. Daniels had told my dad that the reason for Lucy's strange behavior was her need for more attention at home.

"He suggested we all find ways to interact with her more," my dad explained over breakfast this morning. "We need to try some things that she enjoys, focus more on her needs, not ours."

I almost choked on my bran muffin, but I agreed to try. This, though, may be more than I can stand.

"Okay," Lucy says, studying the mass of naked bodies in front of her. She plucks one out of the middle of the row. "They each need something special to wear. You can start with her. She's one of my favorites."

She holds the Barbie out to me, and I take it. I'd be more excited if she'd just handed me her used Kleenex.

"Why is it a favorite?" I ask skeptically. To me, they all look the same: pink, plastic, and blond. "Oh, never mind. Just give me the clothes."

She laughs.

It's the first Sunday of fall break, and I'm bored out of my mind. For two days straight my dad has had us on house arrest.

"Until those boys' tests come back, no one's leaving," he said, looking first at me, then at my mom. "No exceptions, understand?"

We both nodded. "Understand," we said in unison.

"This is the fun part, Charlie!" Lucy holds up a pink wicker basket and turns it upside down. A million pieces of colored fabric rain down on her bed. She looks at me trium-phantly. "You get to pick out their outfits yourself."

"Lucy, you're not serious."

She holds out a bright-orange-and-pink dress.

"Here. She'll look fantastic in this." She drops the dress, then picks up a dark purple one. "Or this one, if you prefer something fancier."

I toss the Barbie onto the bed and stand up. "I've got to clean my room," I tell her.

She looks at me for a minute, then her eyes drop to her lap. She fiddles with the Barbie in her hand, the one with the red sequined ball gown and matching high heels.

"Charlie," she says in an almost-whisper. "No one likes to play with me. The other kids say I'm too bossy." She smooths the doll's hair. "They say Barbies are for babies."

I am not falling for this. "Yeah, well, you are. Bossy, I mean. And they are for babies. Kind of."

She bites her bottom lip.

"Oh jeez," I say, sitting back down. I tap my foot and stare at the ceiling.

"I'm trying, Charlie. I really am," she says. "But I'm a very good leader, and I'm smarter than everyone in my class." She looks up at me. "I wish I was more like you."

"Gee, thanks," I mumble.

"No, really!" Her eyes grow wide. "You're much more"—she

searches for the word—"easygoing. I wish I didn't always have to be in control of everything."

I stare at her. Maybe my bratty sister's human, after all.

"Listen, Lucy," I tell her. "There's nothing wrong with being smart or in control. Just stop rubbing everyone's noses in it all the time."

She nods, biting her lip.

I sigh. "Fine. I'll play for twenty more minutes, but that's it."

"Really?" Her eyes light up like a Christmas tree.

"Yes, really. But I'm not dressing any of them."

She hands me a doll with a sparkly tiara perched on its head. "You can be her. She's the mean one who no one wants to eat lunch with because she steals boyfriends. And she has an eating disorder."

I toss the doll back onto the pile, dislodging her princess crown.

"Fat chance, Lucy."

"Charlie, please . . ."

And then I hear it, my mom's voice from downstairs.

"Burgers! Time for showers!"

Lucy scrunches up her nose. "But it's fall break!" she hollers.

My mom hollers back. "It's also late. Bedtime's in thirty minutes . . . or else!"

I jump up.

"Come on, Charlie," Lucy whines. "Ten more minutes?"

"You heard Mom. Do you really want to find out what 'or else' means?"

I sprint out of the room and toward the bathroom, grinning. Maybe showers aren't so bad, after all.

CHAPTER

33

I'M PLANNING TO SLEEP IN ON MONDAY, BUT I wake up to a buzzing in my ear. I bat at the alarm clock, and it crashes to the ground, but still the buzzing continues. I stuff my head under my pillow, but it's no use. It won't go away.

I sit up and realize it's the doorbell.

I look outside. My mom's squad car has been gone since Friday, but normally the minivan is there. This morning the driveway is empty.

"Okay, okay, calm down," I call out, banging down the stairs. The cold air hits my face the second I pull open the door.

Franki leans against the railing.

"Took you long enough," she says, removing her finger from the buzzer.

"Hi," I say. My chest feels like someone just knocked the

wind out of me. "What're you doing here? Why aren't you in Colorado?"

"Plans fell through," she says. "Even though the snow here didn't amount to much, there was enough in Colorado to cancel most of the flights."

A weird feeling comes over me, and I think back to the journal entry I wrote about Franki.

Did I make this happen?

I shrug, realizing it doesn't matter anymore. The experiment is over. Dude is gone.

And then I realize something else.

"If you weren't in Colorado, then where were you all weekend?"

She kicks at a piece of ice next to the door. "Things got a little heated at my house on Thursday after school. Since I was flying out of Boston the next day, Lila sent me on the train a day early, and I spent the night at Aunt Carol's. When my plane got canceled, I decided to stay for the weekend." She studies the chunk of ice like it's the most interesting thing she's seen all day.

"Franki!" my mom hollers. I turn and see her coming down the stairs.

"You better go," I whisper. "We're on lock-down around here. She'll freak out if—"

My mom grabs Franki's hand. "Why are you standing in the cold?" she asks, pulling her inside. "Come, get warm."

"Mom, I thought no one was allowed in or out until—"

Grinning, she grabs my hand, too. "All the reports are back. Whatever those boys had, it's not contagious, and it's certainly not fatal. In fact, they're being released from the hospital as we speak." She wraps her arms around both of us, smashing our heads together. "See? Everything's going to be just fine."

■ ■ ■

My mom goes upstairs to take a shower, so Franki and I go into the kitchen. I make cinnamon toast and pour orange juice, and Franki sits on the barstool and listens while I fill her in on Thursday's details. I'm just telling her about the fire alarm and how I got everyone out of the building, when she interrupts me, her mouth stuffed with toast.

"I hate him."

I stop pouring the juice and look at her. Franki has some strong opinions, but I've never heard her use *that* word before.

"Come on, Frank. Boomer's done some pretty mean things, but I'm not sure if hating him—"

"Not Boomer." She picks at the crumbs on her plate. "Carl."

Suddenly, my heart starts to beat faster. "Your stepdad?" I ask.

She takes a swig of her juice.

"Franki . . ." I search for something to say. "You want to talk about it?"

"It's not that big of a deal," she says. She sits up straighter. "Can we play Zombie Smasher now?"

We spend the rest of the day sitting in my basement, eating Pop-Tarts and shooting zombies. We even let Lucy join us. Franki doesn't go home until after dinner on Monday, and is on our doorstep before breakfast on Tuesday. By Wednesday, my dad gives her a key so she can let herself in.

It turns out to be a pretty great week.

CHAPTER
34

MY MOM INSISTS ON DRIVING US TO SCHOOL on the first Monday after break.

"But I want to walk," I tell her. "Dad lets me do it all the time."

She looks at me like I just told her I want to wear underwear on my head. "Can you just humor me for once? It's not every day I get a chance to drive you to school, Charles."

Stella floats past us and jumps into the front seat. My older sister would never refuse a ride.

"Fine," I tell her, "but I'm drawing the line at an escort to the bathroom."

When we pull up in front of Gatehouse, we all stare out the windows.

"Business as usual," Stella says.

She's right. The camera trucks, police cars, and reporters are gone. Instead, the courtyard is full of kids stomping their feet and blowing on icy fingers, waiting until the last possible minute before going inside.

I jump out of the van and wave over my shoulder to my mom, who shouts her "have a nice day!" and "be careful!" through the window. My feet crunch across frozen grass as pieces of conversation whip past me and I make my way to the double doors at the top of the stairs. I need to get to the science lab and see Mr. P before the bell rings. I want to tell him that even though I've decided to retire Dude, I'm glad I got to be a part of the whole experiment.

"Hey, kid."

I stop dead, my hand on the door handle. Slowly, I turn and see a guy in a dark-gray hoodie leaning against the brick wall next to me.

A gloved hand motions for me to come closer.

I try to remember what my mom told me about drug pushers—how they lurk outside middle schools and prey on dumb kids who don't know any better. I try to sneak past him, but when he pulls off his hood, I stop in my tracks.

"Calm down," he says as I choke back a scream.

This is no pusher. This is Boomer.

CHAPTER 35

"YOU NEVER CAME BACK TO VISIT."

He stares at me, waiting for an answer. I stare down at his shoes.

"You promised my mom," he growls. "What kind of guy breaks a promise to another guy's mom?"

There's a hole in his left sneaker near his big toe. "Yeah, about that," I say. "I meant to . . . I really did. But things got kind of crazy, and—"

"Shut up, kid." He reaches inside his jacket pocket, and I squeeze my eyes shut. This is it—I'm done for. I hope it's over quick.

"Here," he says. I open my left eye. He's holding out a scrap of paper folded in half. He shakes it at me.

"Take it."

I do and unfold it. Inside is an address that I recognize as being two streets over from Franki's house. I look up and notice a faint smudge of purple still circling Boomer's left eye.

"My mom wants you to come over after school," he says. "She wants us to play chess together."

I take a step back. "You want me to come to your house? Like, to hang out?"

"No, doofus. To play chess." He rolls his eyes. "And maybe eat dinner." He squints at me. "Depending."

"Depending on what?"

He leans forward. "Depending on how much more of a doofus you are."

I fold the paper and stick it into my pocket. "Okay."

He blinks.

"Okay, you'll come?"

I nod. "Yeah. I'll come."

I start to walk past him, but he sinks a meaty hand onto my shoulder. I wince.

"Charlie."

I look up at him, surprised he remembered my name. "Yeah?"

"Not a word of this to anyone. Or else."

I nod and start to open the door, then turn back around.

"All your secrets are safe with me, Sherrel," I say. He stares at me, his mouth hanging open.

I go in the door, grinning. Not bad for a doofus. Not bad at all.

■ ■ ■

I walk into Gatehouse and pass a group of sixth-grade cheerleaders. Today, instead of slinking past them, I glance over. The one with a dark bouncy ponytail smiles at me.

"Hi, Charlie," she says, waving.

"Hi, Emma," I say, hoping my fly isn't open.

"How was your break?" she asks.

"Good. Yours?"

"It was loud." She sighs. "My mom just had a baby, so there was a lot of crying in my house. For something so tiny, he makes a lot of noise."

"Well, if you ever need a place, like, to study or something . . ."

My face flushes hot. Where did that come from?

"Really?" she says, and I notice her eyes light up when she smiles.

"Really."

"Okay," she says. "I'll remember that."

I practically float down the hallway.

As soon as I get to the science lab, my mood takes a nose dive. On the door hangs a note, typed on school letterhead and signed by Dr. Daryl Moody, school principal.

It reads:

Due to an unexpected family emergency, Mr. Maury
Perdzock will be taking an extended leave of absence
for the remainder of the school year.

Please join us in welcoming Nathan Wiseman as
our new sixth-grade science teacher.

I lean up against the wall, then let my body slide down to
the floor.

Mr. P is gone.

Dude is gone.

The experiment is really over.

CHAPTER

36

FRANKI'S SITTING IN HER USUAL SPOT, forking through a glob of creamed corn and peas when I walk into the cafeteria.

"Did you bring it?" She snags my lunch sack out of my hands and starts rooting through it. She whoops and pulls a veggie burger out of my bag. "Do you have any idea how much I've missed these?" She rips open the wrapper and takes a bite.

"You just ate one at my house two days ago."

"I know," she says, her eyes half closed. "But for some reason, they taste better when they're surrounded by crummy cafeteria food."

"Charlie!" I look up as Grant races in. "Did you hear?" His eyebrows disappear into his bangs. "You're not going to believe this."

"Believe what?" Franki says, her mouth full.

"We've made the playoffs." He raises his arms into the air. "We did it! The Gatehouse Vikings are going to the playoffs!"

Franki stops chewing.

"You're joking," I say.

The words tumble out of his mouth. "Dexter just told me. Since we beat the Patriots, it moved us up in the rankings enough to earn a spot. No one's beaten the Patriots for three seasons."

Franki lets out a low whistle. "Not bad, boys."

"Not bad?" Grant squeals. "Not bad? People, this is the best news ever. Do you know what this means?" He grabs the front of my shirt. "We could make it to the championship! We could be district champs! Nobody messes with champs!" He runs circles around the cafeteria, slapping hands and hollering so loud, Dr. Moody threatens to give him detention if he doesn't knock it off.

For the rest of the day, I walk around with a grin so wide, my face hurts.

Wait until my parents hear about this.

CHAPTER

37

"TAKE THE SHOT!"

I'm for sure going to throw up. With only ten seconds left in the Cape Ann District Semifinals, I—Charles Michael Burger, the guy who only plays defense—have no choice but to take the shot.

I dribble toward the goal and try to not think about my stomach. I wish I'd skipped breakfast.

The score is one to one. Maybe if I can just stall for a few more seconds, the game will end in a tie, and we can try to beat them in penalty kicks. Grant lives for penalty kicks.

I look up at the clock: eight seconds left. The Warriors' sweeper moves toward me, his teeth bared. He knows I've never played offense in my life. He zeroes in, waiting for me to make that one mistake—then the ball will be his. Confidence oozes from his pores.

"Charlie! The shot! Take the shot!"

I see the goal but can't get there. I glance to the left and see Grant, but he's in trouble, too. Three Warriors are marking him, wrapped around him like duct tape. They know he's the real threat, not me.

"What're you doing, Burger?" Coach's voice is still squeaky, but he's starting to sound more like his old self. "Stop prancing around and *take the shot!*"

And then I see it . . . my chance. The sweeper's moving toward me—so sure I'm going to screw up that he's willing to leave his goalie unprotected. He crouches, lowering his center of gravity. It's my only chance.

I take a deep breath and head straight toward him. He starts toward me, coming fast—too fast—so I cut to the left, forcing him to move with me. He stabs for the ball, and I pivot to the right. He curses as I fly by.

I'm wide open. Now it's just the goalie and me.

He's in a perfect position, legs splayed, arms out, ready. I glance around one last time, seeing if I can pass the ball off to someone else, but there's no one. Only me.

"Shoot!"

A zap of electricity explodes through my thigh as I pull my leg back. As soon as my foot makes contact with the ball, I look up, knowing exactly where it's headed. It sails through the air, a perfect arch and drops, drops . . .

Bam! The goalkeeper dives, and his fingers bat the ball away. I can't believe it. My one shot . . .

Out of the corner of my eye, I see him. Grant's broken away from the three defenders and is barreling toward the goal. The ball sails toward him, and he heads it, sending it right into the net. The goalie is still on the ground. He never saw it coming.

"We did it!" Grant runs up and throws his arms around my neck as the ref blows his whistle, signaling the end of the game. "We did it, Burger!"

I can't believe it.

We did it!

Our team runs up and joins us as we hoot and holler, chanting over and over again, "Vikings are going to the finals! Vikings are going to the finals!"

Someone grabs me in a headlock and whoops into my ear. I look to the bleachers. My parents wave frantically. There's no sign of my mom's cell phone or my dad's pinched look.

Just two grinning faces that make me feel like a real live superhero.

■ ■ ■

We walk together toward the parking lot, slapping one another's backs, fist-pumping, and screaming like a bunch of five-year-olds. I've never felt a part of something so important, so big.

"Chuck." Even with all the noise, I hear her. Franki leans against the fence that separates the parking lot from the fields. Under the streetlamp, her hair's practically glowing.

I run over to her, forgetting about everyone else.

"Did you see it?" My voice is hoarse. "Did you see the game?"

She fiddles with the zipper on her sweatshirt. "I missed most of it. But I saw your shot."

I hop from one foot to the other, unable to stand still. "So?"

"So?"

The suspense is driving me bonkers. "What'd you think?"

She stops with the zipper and stuffs her hands into her pockets. "I think you were great."

The breeze picks up a piece of her hair, and it floats across her face. My cheeks burn.

"I got to go," she says. "I just wanted to say congratulations."

"Want a ride?" I ask.

She shakes her head. "I feel like walking." She looks over toward the parking lot. "Go back to your team. I'll see you tomorrow."

"Wait," I say as she turns to go. "I'll walk you."

I run over to the van.

"We'll give her a ride," my mom says. "It's cold out here, and you've been sweating for the past—"

"Honey," my dad says softly.

250

"Fine," she says, rolling her eyes at him. She turns back to me. "But no dillydallying, okay?"

"Okay," I tell her. I race back to where I left Franki still glowing under the streetlamp.

■ ■ ■

It's a clear night, and we decide to take the long way, up Beach Street. We can hear the waves lapping the shore as we walk. I quickly point out the Big Dipper, and she finds Orion, something we've done a hundred times before. I fill her in on the parts of the game she missed. She nods but doesn't say much.

"You okay?" I finally ask.

"I don't really want to talk about it," she says. I try to read her face but can't.

We walk for a while in silence.

We get to the bottom of her porch steps. Franki's house is like most houses in her neighborhood: small and square with a postage-stamp yard and a need for a new paint job. A beer bottle leans against the railing, and a rusty tricycle sits off to the side. I can hear the television inside.

"Do you want to sit for a while?" I say.

"Don't you need to get home?"

"I can hang out for a minute or two."

She shrugs and plunks down on the steps, and I do, too. We sit with our backs very straight, our shoulders barely touching. The night feels colder now, and I'm glad I remembered to grab my jacket. Pretty soon she's leaning into me, her body heavy against mine.

After what seems like a long time and no time at all, she stands up. "I got to go. Rose is probably waiting up for me."

I stand up, too.

"Yeah. My mom will send out the cavalry if I'm not—"

She leans toward me and puts her lips on mine. Her eyes squeeze shut.

And then it's over. She turns toward the stairs, taking them two at a time. She pulls open the door and disappears inside.

I stand there for a minute, staring up at the house. Then I start walking home. It's suddenly too warm for a coat.

■ ■ ■

I'm standing in my driveway when I feel them. Goose bumps pop up, covering my skin. At first I think it's because I took off my jacket, but I know that's not it.

Something is wrong.

I look up at my house. There's a light on in Lucy's room, and I can see my dad moving around in the kitchen. The van sits in the driveway, and the porch light is on.

It's Franki. My scalp prickles. Something is wrong with Franki.

I turn and run. Even though it's dark, I cut across Cemetery Hill, not caring about patches of ice or zombies or tree branches. Even when a shadow falls across my path, I don't care. I just run faster.

But when I get to the other side of the cemetery, I stop dead. Even the pounding in my chest freezes midbeat.

I need my science journal. I need Dude Explodius.

I can see the journal, sitting on the tip-top shelf in my closet, where I tucked it away for safekeeping. Just in case.

I want to go back for it, but the prickling feeling starts in my scalp again, and I know I don't have time. Plus, I don't believe in all that superhero stuff anymore, right?

I start running again.

■ ■ ■

I can hear voices, muffled but angry, on the other side of the door.

I stop at the bottom of the steps that lead up to Franki's house. I put my foot on the first stair, hesitating, thinking maybe this isn't such a good idea, after all. Then I hear a crash and a scream.

I stop thinking. I race up the stairs, and I'm almost to the door when my sneaker slips on a piece of ice. My arms are like propellers as I slide across the porch, trying to steady myself. I slam into the door.

"What was that?" I hear from the other side.

I turn the handle before I can change my mind. The door creaks open, and I look around. The light is dim, but it doesn't take me long to see Carl standing in the corner, a beer bottle in his hand. Someone crouches down next to him.

Franki.

"Get away from her!" I scream.

"Charlie?" Franki whispers. "What're you doing here?"

"Get away from her," I say in a voice that's not my own. "I mean it, Carl. Leave her alone, or you're going to be very, very sorry."

"Who're you?" Carl says, his words slurred and slow. "Prince Charming?"

I glance around the room. Pizza boxes and stacks of dishes take up any available space on the couch and coffee table. A television blares in another corner.

I cross the room in three steps and reach around Carl, grabbing ahold of Franki's arm. It takes a little effort, but I pull her into a standing position next to me.

"You okay?" I ask her, and she nods. "Then let's get out of here."

Carl squints at me, his body swaying back and forth. "Playing hero, are you?" He takes a swig of the beer. "I hate to break this to you, buddy, but your little girlfriend ain't going nowhere."

"I'm not your buddy," I tell him, tugging on Franki's arm. She follows me across the living room, but when we reach the door, she stops.

"You're a bad person, Carl," she says, narrowing her eyes at him. "I hope my mom figures that out before it's too late."

Carl sways, then takes a step toward us. "Get back over here. I mean it, girl."

"Let's go!" I holler, pulling her out the door. We slip-slide across the porch, and I grab the banister for balance. We've made it to the first step when I hear him behind us.

"You don't know who you're messing with, kid," he says, coming through the doorway. His face is full of rage, and as he barrels toward us, I shove Franki to the side, moving both of us out of his path. His foot hits an icy patch, and he starts to lose his balance.

"Whoa!" he yells. He smashes into the railing, and we hear a loud snap as he sails through it.

I peek over the side and see him, twisted sideways and motionless, lying on the frozen ground below.

"He's not moving," I whisper.

Franki peers around my shoulder. "Do you think he's dead? I don't really want him to be dead."

We wait, but he just lies there, motionless, drips of melting ice falling on him from the broken gutter above.

"Maybe we should do something," Franki says, and I nod.

"Let's call my mom," I say, turning toward the house. "She'll know what to do."

Franki shakes her head. "Phone's off again."

We make our way down the steps and start heading toward the road, hoping to flag someone down for help. We're almost to her mailbox when the blue minivan comes up the hill and stops next to it.

My mom jumps out of the passenger side.

"Don't get mad," she says to me, holding up her hands. "I'm not trying to treat you like a little kid. It's just that it was getting kind of late, and we wanted to make sure you and Franki made it to her house okay—"

I throw my arms around her neck, and Franki does, too.

"Whoa," my mom says. "What's going on?"

I let go of her. "Mom . . . there's been an accident. Carl— he's hurt and . . ." I motion toward the house but stop when I see him move a little. He tries to roll over, then lets out a wail.

My mom looks at Carl, then at Franki. "You okay?"

"I'm fine, Mrs. Burger. But my mom and Rose. They'll be home soon, and—"

"We'll take care of it." She looks at me. "Charlie, can you walk Franki back to our house? Stella's there with Lucy, and I need your dad to stay here with me."

I nod, and we start walking again. We're halfway down the street when my mom calls out.

"Charles?"

I turn.

"You sure you're okay?"

I nod. "Trust me, Mom. I'm fine."

. . .

Later that night, after Franki's eaten three helpings of my dad's meatless meat loaf and crawled into bed with Lucy, my mom comes into my room. She tells me that Carl's fine, but his right leg is badly broken and he's going to be in a cast for at least twelve weeks.

She smiles at me. "He won't be chasing anyone for a while, that's for sure."

I try to smile back, but my face feels tired, and I can barely keep my eyes open. "I was scared tonight, Mom."

"I know, Charlie. I was too."

"You were?"

"Sure," she says, hugging me. "Nobody's perfect, you know."

I hug her back.

We sit like that for a long time, neither of us wanting to be the first to let go.

CHAPTER

38

I WAKE UP TO MY DAD HOLLERING UP THE stairs.

"Snow day!"

I jump up and peer out the window. At least six new inches cover the backyard. This time, it looks like a real winter wonderland.

I tug a sweatshirt on over my pajama top and go to my closet, searching the top shelf for my wool socks. If we hurry, Franki and I can be at Grant's before the little kids get to the hill.

My hand grazes the familiar leather of my science journal. Tiny bolts of electricity shoot up my fingers.

I pull it out and hold it up to my nose, inhaling the now-faded smell of rawhide and thinking about Mr. P.

I hope, wherever he is, he keeps doing his experiment. Even when it got messy, it was worth it.

■ ■ ■

I peer into Lucy's room. Her bedspread is pulled up tight, and her five billion stuffed animals are lined up like always. She sits in the middle of them, her Barbies spread all around.

"Where's Franki?" I ask her.

"She promised she was going to play with me this morning," she says to me, not looking up. "You want to play instead?"

Fat chance, I think, but bite the inside of my cheek so the words won't come out.

"Maybe later," I say as I run down the stairs, hoping she's in the kitchen.

As I'm passing the front hallway, the doorbell buzzes.

"Got it!" I scream, and unlock the door. I pull it open, and Franki stands in front of me, wearing a parka plus a pair of thick gloves and a stocking cap.

I grin up at her. "I just need to eat a quick breakfast, then I'm ready to go." I look behind her. "Did you go home to get your sled?"

"Charlie . . ."

I sigh. If we have to go all the way back to her house, it's going to eat up another twenty minutes. "Fine. You can borrow Lucy's. She's busy anyway."

Franki gives me a look that makes me think she's not thinking about sleds or Cemetery Hill.

"Didn't your mom tell you?"

"Tell me what?" My stomach growls.

"I'm . . . I'm going away."

Not this again. "What do you mean . . . like, to visit your dad?"

She nods and slides her high-top along a patch of powdery snow. "Yeah. Lila and your mom worked it all out with my dad. They say it's for the best."

"They say what's for the best?"

She shifts from one foot to the next. "I might be going away for a while. At least until after Christmas."

When I went to bed last night, Franki was curled up next to Lucy, snoring like a truck driver. Now she's telling me she's leaving, maybe for more than just a week. I take a deep breath, and frosty air fills my lungs.

"So, when do you go?"

"Today."

I shake my head. This can't be happening. Not now.

"Lila took some time off, so we're all driving to Boston this afternoon. We're going to stay with Aunt Carol for a few days, and then I'll fly to Colorado."

I try to breathe, but the air burns at my insides.

"Don't be sad, Charlie. It's not forever."

"Nothing's ever forever," I say.

"We'll sled when I come back," she says, her face lighting up.

"Okay." It's the most I can manage.

We stand like that for a minute. Finally, she looks down at me and gives me a gentle shove.

"Well, then," she says, "I guess I'll say Merry Christmas now."

I nod.

She turns and starts down the steps.

"Frank?"

She whips around.

"Yeah?"

I take one more deep breath. "We'll sled when you come back."

The lopsided grin spreads like maple syrup across her freckly face.

"You can count on it, Charlie Burger."

CHAPTER
39

FRANKI DOESN'T COME BACK IN TIME TO GO sledding.

After she left for Colorado, things got pretty bad between Lila and Carl. He couldn't do much for himself, on account of his broken leg, so Lila took pity on him and came back from Boston to take care of him. Everything was pretty calm for about a week.

My mom wouldn't give me all the details but said Carl's actions eventually landed him a spot in jail overnight and convinced Lila to take Rose and go back to Boston for good. Two weeks later a FOR SALE sign went up in their yard.

At first, Franki and I wrote to each other all the time. I told her about how Boomer's mom makes the best chicken-fried steak and how he got two other guys to join the chess club without even bullying them into doing it. I filled her in on Grant and Dolores's love affair, and how even though our soccer team didn't win the finals, Coach Crenshaw made it through the whole game without making a single guy puke or cry. I told her about my mom's decision to retire from the police force for good, and how she's trying to convince my dad to open his own restaurant. I even told her about how Lucy talked me into showing her how to hunt for frogs at Mill Pond, and how Stella already got elected to be president of her class for next year.

She told me about Colorado, her stepmom and half brothers, and how she's learning to ski. She wrote about her new school and the debate team and some of the friends she's made. She wrote about her dad, and how much he likes soccer and playing the guitar and old show tunes, just like Pickles.

But by March, her letters weren't coming as much, and by April, they stopped altogether. Then one night in early May, I got home from play practice, and my mom said she had called.

"Here's her number," she said, holding out a piece of paper. "I told her you'd call as soon as you got home."

I grabbed it and ran up the stairs. Dolores had invited Emma and me to come over and study with her and Grant, and I didn't want to be late. But I had to call Franki first.

A little boy picked up on the first ring.

"Hello! Austin's house!"

"Hi, may I speak to Franki?"

He giggled. "Who are you?"

"Umm." I thought for a few seconds. "I'm her friend. Charlie. Charlie Burger."

"Charlie Booger?" He giggled harder. "That's a funny name."

"Burger," I said again. "Can I just talk to Franki, please?"

"Like a hamburger?" He paused for a minute. "I like hamburgers."

I couldn't help but grin. "I am her friend calling from far away. Could you please just put her on the phone?"

He got quiet for a minute, and I thought he'd gone to get her. Then, "Franki's gone."

My heart skipped a beat. "Where did she go?"

He giggled again. "Out. With friends. But not Charlie Hamburger."

I hung up and stuffed the piece of paper into my pocket.

A couple of days later, I tried again.

"Hello! Austin's house!"

I think the number ended up in the wash, because after that, I couldn't find it again.

And now here it is—lunchtime on the last day of sixth grade, and I'm sprinting through the courtyard. I've promised Emma I'd help her hang the banner announcing the after-school beach party, and I told Coach I'd help him gather the guys for an end-of-year meeting. He wants to give us his don't-turn-into-a-bunch-of-cream-puffs-over-summer lecture.

I'm halfway across the yard when I see her. She walks toward me, her bright-green high-tops the first thing I recognize.

The only thing, really. Because even though it's Franki, it's not *my* Franki. Not really. Not anymore.

"Charlie!" She breaks into a run.

"Frank?"

She throws her arms around my neck and squeezes so hard, I think my head's going to pop off.

"You're taller," she says, and I grin. We look at each other, eye to eye.

She's changed, too. Her hair is shorter, just grazing her shoulders. Her clothes no longer hang off her, and my face flushes when I notice bumps where she never had any before. Her face has fewer freckles, and tiny gold hoops dangle from her ears.

My dad would say she's turned into a looker.

I don't want to stare, but I can't stop. Her eyes hold on to mine, twinkling like she's about to tell me one of her dirty jokes.

"What are you doing here?" I ask. Wow, do I sound like a dope.

But she just grins. "School got out last week, and I flew to Boston to spend the summer with Lila and Rose. We decided to take the train up this morning to visit some old friends. Lila said I could come by and surprise you."

"Oh." I scuff my worn-out sneakers on the pavement and study the hole in the right toe.

"I can't believe sixth grade's over," she says. "It feels like it just started."

I nod. "It's been a pretty crazy year."

"It's been a pretty crazy year," she repeats.

Her face turns serious. "Can we meet after school? We could go to your house first so I can say hi to your family. Then we could go to the beach. The tide's low, and there aren't any tourists yet." She talks faster. "We'll take your pails and maybe some veggie burgers left over from today's lunch rush?" She slugs me in the arm. "Come on, Chuck. It'll be like old times."

I think about Franki and me, and how long we've been friends. I think about the Dinosaur Crunch ice cream cones and the games of Zombie Smasher. But mostly I think about what Stella told me, all the way back last summer, about how things were going to be different for Franki and me once we started middle school. I think about all this as I look at her now, with her short hair and hoop earrings, and I know she needs me to remind her that no matter how much things change, some things will always stay the same.

She grabs my hand, and my stomach flips over, like before.

"I'll meet you right here," I say.

And then, without thinking, I lean over and press my lips against her cheek, right below her eye. Her skin is warm and still smells like syrup.

And then I take off.

Emma's waiting for me, and I can't afford to be tardy just because Franki Saylor wants to stand around and hold my hand all day.